J. G. Ballard was born in 1930 in Shanghai, China, where his father was a businessman. Afte  Ballard and his family were pla They returned to England i Cambridge, where he read m copywriter and Covent Garden with the RAF. In 1956 his first *New Worlds* and he took a full-ti where he stayed until 1961. His first novel, *The Drowned World*, was written in the same year. His novel *Empire of the Sun* won the Guardian Fiction Prize and the James Tait Black Award, and was filmed by Steven Spielberg.

By the same author

Novels

Short Stories

J. G. BALLARD

The Disaster Area

Paladin
An Imprint of HarperCollins*Publishers*

Paladin
An Imprint of HarperCollins*Publishers*
77–85 Fulham Palace Road,
Hammersmith, London W6 8JB

Published by Paladin 1992
9 8 7 6 5 4 3 2 1

Previously published by
Triad/Panther Books 1979
Reprinted 1985

First published in Great Britain by
Jonathan Cape Ltd 1967

ISBN 0 586 09071 1

Printed in Great Britain by
HarperCollinsManufacturing Glasgow

Contents

The Disaster Area

At dawn the bodies of the dead birds shone in the damp light of the marsh, their grey plumage hanging in the still water like fallen clouds. Each morning when Crispin went out on to the deck of the picket ship he would see the birds lying in the creeks and waterways where they had died two months earlier, their wounds cleansed now by the slow current, and he would watch the white-haired woman who lived in the empty house below the cliff walking by the river. Along the narrow beach the huge birds, larger than condors, lay at her feet. As Crispin gazed at her from the bridge of the picket ship she moved among them, now and then stooping to pluck a feather from the outstretched wings. At the end of her walk, when she returned across the damp meadow to the empty house, her arms would be loaded with immense white plumes.

At first Crispin had felt an obscure sense of annoyance at the way this strange woman descended on to the beach and calmly plundered the plumage of the dead birds. Although many thousands of the creatures lay along the margins of the river and in the marshes around the inlet where the picket ship was moored, Crispin still maintained a proprietary attitude towards them. He himself, almost single-handedly, had been responsible for the slaughter of the birds in the last terrifying battles when they had come from their eyries along the North Sea and attacked the picket ship. Each of the immense white creatures—for the most part gulls and gannets, with a few fulmars and petrels—carried *his* bullet in its heart like a jewel.

As he watched the woman cross the overgrown lawn to her house Crispin remembered again the frantic hours before the birds' final hopeless attack. Hopeless it seemed now, when their bodies lay in a wet quilt over the cold

Norfolk marshes, but then, only two months earlier, when the sky above the ship had been dark with their massing forms, it was Crispin who had given up hope.

The birds had been larger than men, with wing spans of twenty feet or more that shut out the sun. Crispin had raced like a madman across the rusty metal decks, dragging the ammuntion cans in his torn arms from the armoury and loading them into the breeches of the machine-guns, while Quimby, the idiot youth from the farm at Long Reach whom Crispin had persuaded to be his gun loader, gibbered to himself on the foredeck, hopping about on his club foot as he tried to escape from the huge shadows sweeping across him. When the birds began their first dive, and the sky turned into a white scythe, Crispin had barely enough time to buckle himself into the shoulder harness of the turret.

Yet he had won, shooting the first wave down into the marshes as they soared towards him like a white armada, then turning to fire at the second group swooping in low across the river behind his back. The hull of the picket ship was still dented with the impacts their bodies had made as they struck the sides above the waterline. At the height of the battle the birds had been everywhere, wings like screaming crosses against the sky, their corpses crashing through the rigging on to the decks around him as he swung the heavy guns, firing from rail to rail. A dozen times Crispin had given up hope, cursing the men who had left him alone on this rusty hulk to face the giant birds, and who made him pay for Quimby out of his own pocket.

But then, when the battle had seemed to last for ever, when the sky was still full of birds and his ammunition had nearly gone, he noticed Quimby dancing on the corpses heaped on the deck, pitching them into the water with his two-pronged fork as they thudded around him.

Then Crispin knew that he had won. When the firing

slackened Quimby dragged up more ammunition, eager for killing, his face and deformed chest smeared with feathers and blood. Shouting himself now, with a fierce pride in his own courage and fear, Crispin had destroyed the remainder of the birds, shooting the stragglers, a few fledgling peregrines, as they fled towards the cliff. For an hour after the last of the birds had died, when the river and the creeks near the ship ran red with their blood, Crispin had sat in the turret, firing the guns at the sky that had dared attack him.

Later, when the excitement and pulse of the battle had passed, he realized that the only witness of his stand against this aerial armageddon had been a club-footed idiot to whom no one would ever listen. Of course, the white-haired woman had been there, hiding behind the shutters in her house, but Crispin had not noticed her until several hours had passed, when she began to walk among the corpses. To begin with, therefore, he had been glad to see the birds lying where they had fallen, their blurred forms eddying away in the cold water of the river and the marshes. He sent Quimby back to his farm, and watched the idiot dwarf punt his way down-river among the swollen corpses. Then, crossed bandoliers of machine-gun cartridges around his chest, Crispin took command of his bridge.

The woman's appearance on the scene he welcomed, glad someone else was there to share his triumph, and well aware that she must have noticed him patrolling the captain's walk of the picket ship. But after a single glance the woman never again looked at him. She seemed intent only on searching the beach and the meadow below her house.

On the third day after the battle she had come out on to the lawn with Quimby, and the dwarf spent the morning and afternoon clearing away the bodies of the birds that had fallen there. He heaped them on to a heavy wooden tumbril, then harnessed himself between the shafts and dragged them away to a pit near the farm. The following day he appeared again in a wooden skiff and punted the woman, standing alone in the bows like an aloof wraith, among the bodies of the birds floating in the water. Now and then Quimby turned one of the huge corpses over with his pole, as if searching for something among them—there were apocryphal stories, which many townsfolk believed, that the beaks of the birds carried tusks of ivory, but Crispin knew this to be non-sense.

These movements of the women puzzled Crispin, who felt that his conquest of the birds had also tamed the landscape around the picket ship and everything in it. Shortly afterwards, when the woman began to collect the wing feathers of the birds, he felt that she was in some way usurping a privilege reserved for him alone. Sooner or later the river voles, rats and other predators of the marshes would destroy the birds, but until then he resented anyone else looting this drowned treasure which he had won so hard. After the battle he had sent a short message in his crabbed handwriting to the district officer at the station twenty miles away, and until a reply came he preferred that the thousands of bodies should lie where they had fallen. As a conscripted member of the picket service he was not eligible for a bounty, but Crispin dimly hoped he might receive a medal or some sort of commendation.

The knowledge that the woman was his only witness, apart from the idiot Quimby, deterred Crispin from doing anything that might antagonize her. Also, the woman's odd behaviour made Crispin suspect that she too might be mad. He had never seen her at a shorter distance than the three hundred yards separating the picket ship from the bank below her house, but through the telescope mounted on the rail of the bridge he followed her along the beach, and saw more clearly the white hair and the ashen skin of her high face. Her arms were thin but strong, hands held at her waist as she moved about in a grey ankle-length robe. Her bedraggled appearance was that of someone unaware that she had lived alone for a long time.

For several hours Crispin watched her walking among the corpses. The tide cast a fresh freight on to the sand each day, but now that the bodies were decomposing their appearance, except at a distance, was devoid of any sentiment. The shallow inlet in which the picket ship was moored—the vessel was one of the hundreds of old coastal freighters hastily converted to duty when the first flocks of giant birds appeared two years earlier—faced the house across the river. Through the telescope Crispin could count the scores of pockmarks in the white stucco where spent bullets from his guns had lodged themselves.

At the end of her walk the woman had filled her arms with a garland of feathers. As Crispin watched, hands clasping the bandoliers across his chest, she went over to one of the birds, walking into the shallow water to peer into its half-submerged face. Then she plucked a single plume from its wing and added it to the collection in her arms.

Restlessly Crispin returned to the telescope. In the narrow eyepiece her swaying figure, almost hidden by the spray of white feathers, resembled that of some huge decorative bird, a white peacock. Perhaps in some bizarre way she imagined she was a bird?

In the wheelhouse Crispin fingered the signal pistol fastened to the wall. When she came out the next morning he could fire one of the flares over her head, warning her that the birds were his, subjects of his own transitory kingdom. The farmer, Hassell, who had come with Quimby for permission to burn some of the birds for use as fertilizer, had plainly acknowledged Crispin's moral rights over them.

Usually Crispin made a thorough inspection of the ship each morning, counting the ammunition cases and checking the gunnery mountings. The metal caissons were splitting the rusty decks. The whole ship was settling into the mud below. At high tide Crispin would listen to the water pouring through a thousand cracks and rivet holes like an army of silver-tongued rats.

This morning, however, his inspection was brief. After testing the turret on the bridge—there was always the chance of a few stragglers appearing from the nesting grounds along the abandoned coast—he went back to his telescope. The woman was somewhere behind the house, cutting down the remains of a small rose pergola. Now and then she would look up at the sky and at the cliff above, scanning the dark line of the escarpment as if waiting for one of the birds.

This reminder that he had overcome his own fears of the giant birds made Crispin realize why he resented the woman plucking their feathers. As their bodies and plumage began to dissolve he felt a growing need to preserve them. Often he found himself thinking of their great tragic faces as they swooped down upon him, in many ways more to be pitied than feared, victims of what the district officer had called a 'biological accident'—Crispin vaguely remembered him describing the new growth promoters used on the crops in East Anglia and the extraordinary and unforeseen effects on the bird life.

Five years earlier Crispin had been working in the fields as a labourer, unable to find anything better after his wasted years of military service. He remembered the first of the new sprays being applied to the wheat and fruit crops, and the tacky phosphorescent residue that made them glimmer in the moonlight, transforming the placid agricultural backwater into a strange landscape where the forces of some unseen nature were for ever gathering themselves in readiness. The fields had been covered with the dead bodies of gulls and magpies whose mouths were clogged with this silvering gum. Crispin himself had saved many of the half-conscious birds, cleaning their beaks and feathers, and sending them off to their sailing grounds along the coast.

Three years later the birds had returned. The first giant cormorants and black-headed gulls had wing spans of ten or twelve feet, strong bodies and beaks that could slash a dog apart, Soaring low over the fields as Crispin drove his tractor under the empty skies, they seemed to be waiting for something.

The next autumn a second generation of even larger birds appeared, sparrows as fierce as eagles, gannets and gulls with the wing spans of condors. These immense creatures, with bodies as broad and powerful as a man's, flew out of the storms along the coast, killing the cattle in the fields and attacking the farmers and their families. Returning for some reason to the infected crops that had given them this wild spur to growth, they were the advance guard of an aerial armada of millions of birds that filled the skies over the country. Driven by hunger, they began to attack the human beings who were their only source of food.

Crispin had been too busy defending the farm where he lived to follow the course of the battle against the birds all over the world. The farm, only ten miles from the coast, had been besieged. After the dairy cattle had been slaughtered, the birds turned to the farm buildings. One night Crispin woke as a huge frigate bird, its shoulders wider than a door, had shattered the wooden shutters across his window and thrust itself into his room. Seizing his pitchfork, Crispin nailed it by the neck to the wall.

After the destruction of the farm, in which the owner, his family and three of the labourers died. Crispin volunteered to join the picket service. The district officer who headed the motorized militia column at first refused Crispin's offer of help. Surveying the small, ferret-like man with his beaked nose and the birthmark like a star below his left eye, hobbling in little more than a blood-streaked singlet across the wreck of the farmhouse, as the last of the birds wheeled away like giant crosses, the district officer had shaken his head, seeing in Crispin's eyes only the blind hunt for revenge.

However, when they counted the dead birds around the brick kiln where Crispin had made his stand, armed only with a scythe a head taller than himself, the officer had taken him on. He was given a rifle, and for half an hour they moved through the shattered fields near by, filled with the stripped skeletons of cattle and pigs, finishing off the wounded birds that lay there.

Finally, Crispin had come to the picket ship, a drab hulk rusting in a backwater of riverine creeks and marshes, where a dwarf punted his coracle among the dead birds and a mad woman bedecked herself on the beach with garlands of feathers.

For an hour Crispin paced round the ship, as the woman worked behind the house. At one point she appeared with a laundry basket filled with feathers and spread them out on a trestle table beside the rose pergola.

At the stern of the ship Crispin kicked open the galley door. He peered into the murky interior.

'Quimby! Are you there?'

This damp hovel was still maintained as a home from home by Quimby. The dwarf would pay sudden visits to Crispin, presumably in the hope of seeing further action against the birds.

When there was no reply Crispin shouldered his rifle

and made for the gangway. Still eyeing the opposite shore, where a small fire was now sending a plume of grey smoke into the placid air, he tightened his bandoliers and stepped down the creaking gangway to the launch at the bottom.

The dead bodies of the birds were massed around the picket ship in a soggy raft. After trying to drive the launch through them Crispin stopped the outboard motor and seized the gaff. Many of the birds weighed as much as five hundred pounds, lying in the water with their wings interlocked, tangled up with the cables and rope tossed down from the decks. Crispin could barely push them apart with the gaff, and slowly forced the launch to the mouth of the inlet.

He remembered the district officer telling him that the birds were closely related to the reptiles—evidently this explained their blind ferocity and hatred of the mammals—but to Crispin their washed faces in the water looked more like those of drowned dolphins, almost manlike in their composed and individual expressions. As he made his way across the river past the drifting forms it seemed to him that he had been attacked by a race of winged men, driven on not by cruelty or blind instinct but by a sense of some unknown and irrevocable destiny. Along the opposite bank the silver forms of the birds lay among the trees and on the open patches of grass. As he sat in the launch on the water the landscape seemed to Crispin like the morning after some apocalyptic battle of the heavens, the corpses like those of fallen angels.

He moored the launch by the beach, pushing aside the dead birds lying in the shallows. For some reason a flock of pigeons, a few doves among them, had fallen at the water's edge. Their plump-breasted bodies, at least ten feet from head to tail, lay as if asleep on the damp sand, eyes closed in the warm sunlight. Holding his bandoliers to prevent them slipping off his shoulders, Crispin climbed the bank. Ahead lay a small meadow filled with corpses. He walked through them towards the house, now and then treading on the wing tips.

A wooden bridge crossed a ditch into the grounds of the house. Beside it, like a heraldic symbol pointing his way, reared the up-ended wing of a white eagle. The immense plumes with their exquisite modelling reminded him of monumental sculpture, and in the slightly darker light as he approached the cliff the apparent preservation of the birds' plumage made the meadow resemble a vast avian mortuary garden.

As he rounded the house the woman was standing by the trestle table, laying out more feathers to dry. To her left, beside the frame of the gazebo, was what Crispin at first assumed to be a bonfire of white feathers, piled on to a crude wooden framework she had built from the remains of the pergola. An air of dilapidation hung over the house—most of the windows had been broken by the birds during their attacks over the past years, and the garden and yard were filled with litter.

The woman turned to face Crispin. To his surprise she gazed at him with a hard eye, unimpressed by the brigand-like appearance he presented with his cartridge bandoliers, rifle and scarred face. Through the telescope he had guessed her to be elderly, but in fact she was barely more than thirty years old, her white hair as thick and well groomed as the plumage of the dead birds in the fields around them. The rest of her, however, despite the strong figure and firm hands, was as neglected as the house. Her handsome face, devoid of all make up, seemed to have been deliberately exposed to the cutting winter winds, and the long woollen robe she wore was stained with oil, its frayed hem revealing a pair of worn sandals.

Crispin came to a halt in front of her, for a moment

wondering why he was visiting her at all. The few bales of feathers heaped on the pyre and drying on the trestle table seemed no challenge to his authority over the birds —the walk across the meadow had more than reminded him of that. Yet he was aware that something, perhaps their shared experience of the birds, bonded him and the young woman. The empty killing sky, the freighted fields silent in the sun, and the pyre beside them imposed a sense of a common past.

Laying the last of the feathers on the trestle, the woman said, 'They'll dry soon. The sun is warm today. Can you help me?'

Crispin moved forward uncertainly. 'How do you mean? Of course.'

The woman pointed to a section of the rose pergola that was still standing. A rusty saw was embedded in a small groove the woman had managed to cut in one of the uprights. 'Can you cut that down for me?'

Crispin followed her over to the pergola, unslinging his rifle. He pointed to the remains of a pine fence that had collapsed to one side of the old kitchen garden. 'You want wood? That'll burn better.'

'No—I need this frame. It's got to be strong.' She hesitated as Crispin continued to fiddle with his rifle, her voice more defensive. 'Can you do it? The little dwarf couldn't come today. He usually helps me.'

Crispin raised a hand to silence her. 'I'll help you.' He leaned his rifle against the pergola and took hold of the saw, after a few strokes freed it from its groove and made a clean start.

'Thank you.' As he worked the woman stood beside him, looking down with a friendly smile as the cartridge bandoliers began to flap rhythmically to the motion of his arm and chest.

Crispin stopped, reluctant to shed the bandoliers of machine-gun bullets, the badge of his authority. He glanced in the direction of the picket ship, and the woman, taking her cue, said, 'You're the captain? I've seen you on the bridge.'

'Well . . .' Crispin had never heard himself described as the vessel's captain, but the title seemed to carry a certain status. He nodded modestly. 'Crispin,' he said by way of introduction. 'Captain Crispin. Glad to help you.'

'I'm Catherine York.' Holding her white hair to her neck with one hand, the woman smiled again. She pointed to the rusting hulk. 'It's a fine ship.'

Crispin worked away at the saw, wondering whether she was missing the point. When he carried the frame over to the pyre and laid it at the base of the feathers he replaced his bandoliers with calculated effect. The woman appeared not to notice, but a moment later, when she glanced up at the sky, he raised his rifle and went up to her.

'Did you see one? Don't worry, I'll get it.' He tried to follow her eyes as they swept across the sky after some invisible object that seemed to vanish beyond the cliff, but she turned away and began to adjust the feathers mechanically. Crispin gestured at the fields around them, feeling his pulse beat again at the prospect and fear of battle. 'I shot all these . . .'

'What? I'm sorry, what did you say?' The woman looked around. She appeared to have lost interest in Crispin and was vaguely waiting for him to leave.

'Do you want more wood?' Crispin asked. 'I can get some.'

'I have enough.' She touched the feathers on the trestle, then thanked Crispin and walked off into the house, closing the hall door on its rusty hinges.

Crispin made his way across the lawn and through the meadow. The birds lay around him as before, but the memory, however fleeting, of the woman's sympathetic smile made him ignore them. He set off in the launch, pushing away the floating birds with brusque motions of the gaff. The picket ship sat at its moorings, the soggy raft of grey corpses around it. For once the rusting hulk depressed Crispin.

As he climbed the gangway he saw Quimby's small figure on the bridge, wild eyes roving about at the sky. Crispin had expressly forbidden the dwarf to be near the steering helm, though there was little likelihood of the picket ship going anywhere. Irritably he shouted at Quimby to get off the ship.

The dwarf leaped down the threadbare network of ratlines to the deck. He scurried over to Crispin.

'Crisp!' he shouted in his hoarse whisper. 'They saw one! Coming in from the coast! Hassell told me to warn you.'

Crispin stopped. Heart pounding, he scanned the sky out of the sides of his eyes, at the same time keeping a close watch on the dwarf. 'When?'

'Yesterday.' The dwarf wriggled one shoulder, as if trying to dislodge a stray memory. 'Or was it this morning? Anyway, it's coming. Are you ready, Crisp?'

Crispin walked past, one hand firmly on the breech of his rifle. 'I'm always ready,' he rejoined. 'What about you?' He jerked a finger at the house. 'You should have been with the woman. Catherine York. I had to help her. She said she didn't want to see you again.'

'What?' The dwarf scurried about, hands dancing along the rusty rail. He gave up with an elaborate shrug. 'Ah, she's a strange one. Lost her man, you know, Crisp. And her baby.'

Crispin paused at the foot of the bridge companionway. 'Is that right? How did it happen?'

'A dove killed the man, pulled him to pieces on the roof, then took the baby. A tame bird, mark you.' He nodded when Crispin looked at him sceptically. 'That's it. He was another strange one, that York. Kept this big

21

dove on a chain.'

Crispin climbed on to the bridge and stared across the river at the house. After musing to himself for five minutes he kicked Quimby off the ship, and then spent half an hour checking the gunnery installation. The reported sighting of one of the birds he discounted—no doubt a few strays were still flitting about, searching for their flocks—but the vulnerability of the woman across the river reminded him to take every precaution. Near the house she would be relatively safe, but in the open, during her walks along the beach, she would be an all too easy prey.

It was this undefined feeling of responsibility towards Catherine York that prompted him, later that afternoon, to take the launch out again. A quarter of a mile down-river he moored the craft by a large open meadow, directly below the flight path of the birds as they had flown in to attack the picket ship. Here, on the cool green turf, the dying birds had fallen most thickly. A recent fall of rain concealed the odour of the immense gulls and fulmars lying across each other like angels. In the past Crispin had always moved with pride among this white harvest he had reaped from the sky, but now he hurried down the winding aisles between the birds, a wicker basket under his arm, intent only on his errand.

When he reached the higher ground in the centre of the meadow he placed the basket on the carcass of a dead falcon and began to pluck the feathers from the wings and breasts of the birds lying about him. Despite the rain, the plumage was almost dry. Crispin worked steadily for half an hour, tearing out the feathers with his hands, then carried the basketfuls of plumes down to the launch. As he scurried about the meadow his bent head and shoulders were barely visible above the corpses of the birds.

By the time he set off in the launch the small craft

was loaded from bow to stern with the bright plumes. Crispin stood in the steering well, peering over his cargo as he drove up-river. He moored the boat on the beach below the woman's house. A thin trail of smoke rose from the fire, and he could hear Mrs York chopping more kindling.

Crispin walked through the shallow water around the boat, selecting the choicest of the plumes and arranging them around the basket—a falcon's brilliant tail feathers, the mother-of-pearl plumes of a fulmar, the brown breast feathers of an eider. Shouldering the basket, he set off towards the house.

Catherine York was moving the trestle closer to the fire, straightening the plumes as the smoke drifted past them. More feathers had been added to the pyre built on to the frame of the pergola. The outer ones had been woven together to form a firm rim.

Crispin put the basket down in front of her, then stood back. 'Mrs York, I brought these. I thought you might use them.'

The woman glanced obliquely at the sky, then shook her head as if puzzled. Crispin suddenly wondered if she recognized him. 'What are they?'

'Feathers. For over there.' Crispin pointed at the pyre. 'They're the best I could find.'

Catherine York knelt down, her skirt hiding the scuffed sandals. She touched the coloured plumes as if recalling their original owners. 'They are beautiful. Thank you, captain.' She stood up. 'I'd like to keep them, but I need only this kind.'

Crispin followed her hand as she pointed to the white feathers on the trestle. With a curse, he slapped the breech of the rifle.

'Doves! They're all doves! I should have noticed!' He picked up the basket. 'I'll get you some.'

'Crispin . . .' Catherine York took his arm. Her

troubled eyes wandered about his face, as if hoping to find some kindly way of warning him off. 'I have enough, thank you. It's nearly finished now.'

Crispin hesitated, waiting for himself to say something to this beautiful white-haired woman whose hands and robe were covered with the soft down of the doves. Then he picked up the basket and made his way back to the launch.

As he sailed across the river to the ship he moved up and down the launch, casting the cargo of feathers on to the water. Behind him, the soft plumes formed a wake.

That night, as Crispin lay in his rusty bunk in the captain's cabin, his dreams of the giant birds who filled the moonlit skies of his sleep were broken by the faint ripple of the air in the rigging overhead, the muffled hoot of an aerial voice calling to itself. Waking, Crispin lay still with his head against the metal stanchion, listening to the faint whoop and swerve around the mast.

Crispin leaped from the bunk. He seized his rifle and raced barefoot up the companionway to the bridge. As he stepped on to the deck, sliding the barrel of the rifle into the air, he caught a last glimpse against the moonlit night of a huge white bird flying away across the river.

Crispin rushed to the rail, trying to steady the rifle enough to get in a shot at the bird. He gave up as it passed beyond his range, its outline masked by the cliff. Once warned, the bird would never return to the ship. A stray, no doubt it was hoping to nest among the masts and rigging.

Shortly before dawn, after a ceaseless watch from the rail, Crispin set off across the river in the launch. Overexcited, he was convinced he had seen it circling above the house. Perhaps it had seen Catherine York asleep through one of the shattered windows. The muffled echo of the engine beat across the water, broken by the floating forms of the dead birds. Crispin crouched forward with the rifle and drove the launch on to the beach. He ran through the darkened meadow, where the corpses lay like silver shadows. He darted into the cobbled yard and knelt by the kitchen door, trying to catch the sounds of the sleeping woman in the room above.

For an hour, as the dawn lifted over the cliff, Crispin prowled around the house. There were no signs of the bird, but at last he came across the mound of feathers mounted on the pergola frame. Peering into the soft grey bowl, he realized that he had caught the dove in the very act of building a nest.

Careful not to waken the woman sleeping above him beyond the cracked panes, he destroyed the nest. With his rifle butt he stove in the sides, then knocked a hole through the woven bottom. Then, happy that he had saved Catherine York from the nightmare of walking from her house the next morning and seeing the bird waiting to attack her from its perch on this stolen nest, Crispin set off through the gathering light and returned to the ship.

For the next two days, despite his vigil on the bridge, Crispin saw no more of the dove. Catherine York remained within the house, unaware of her escape. At night, Crispin would patrol her house. The changing weather, and the first taste of the winter to come, had unsettled the landscape, and during the day Crispin spent more time upon the bridge, uneager to look out on the marshes that surrounded the ship.

On the night of the storm, Crispin saw the bird again. All afternoon the dark clouds had come in from the sea along the river basin, and by evening the cliff beyond the house was hidden by the rain. Crispin was in the bridge-house, listening to the bulkheads groaning as the ship was driven farther into the mud by the wind.

Lightning flickered across the river, lighting the thousands of corpses in the meadows. Crispin leaned on the helm, gazing at the gaunt reflection of himself in the darkened glass, when a huge white face, beaked like his own, swam into his image. As he stared at this apparition, a pair of immense white wings seemed to unfurl themselves from his shoulders. Then this lost dove, illuminated in a flicker of lightning, rose into the gusting wind around the mast, its wings weaving themselves among the steel cables.

It was still hovering there, trying to find shelter from the rain, when Crispin stepped on to the deck and shot it through the heart.

At first light Crispin left the bridge-house and climbed on to the roof. The dead bird hung, its wings outstretched, in a clutter of steel coils beside the lookout's nest. Its mournful face gaped down at Crispin, its expression barely changed since it loomed out of his own reflection at the height of the storm. Now, as the flat wind faded across the water, Crispin watched the house below the cliff. Against the dark vegetation of the meadows and marshes the bird hung like a white cross, and he waited for Catherine York to come to a window, afraid that a sudden gust might topple the dove to the deck.

When Quimby arrived in his coracle two hours later, eager to see the bird, Crispin sent him up the mast to secure the dove to the cross-tree. Dancing about beneath the bird, the dwarf seemed mesmerized by Crispin, doing whatever the latter told him.

'Fire a shot at her, Crisp!' he exhorted Crispin, who stood disconsolately by the rail. 'Over the house, that'll bring her out!'

'Do you think so?' Crispin raised the rifle, ejecting the cartridge whose bullet had destroyed the bird. He watched the bright shell tumble down into the feathery water below. 'I don't know . . . it might frighten her. I'll go over there.'

'That's the way, Crisp . . .' The dwarf scuttled about. 'Bring her back here—I'll tidy it up for you.'

'Maybe I will.'

As he berthed the launch on the beach Crispin looked back at the picket ship, reassuring himself that the dead dove was clearly visible in the distance. In the morning sunlight the plumage shone like snow against the rusting masts.

When he neared the house he saw Catherine York standing in the doorway, her wind-blown hair hiding her face, watching him approach with stern eyes.

He was ten yards from her when she stepped into the house and half closed the door. Crispin began to run, and she leaned out and shouted angrily : 'Go away! Go back to the ship and those dead birds you love so much!'

'Miss Catherine . . .' Crispin stammered to a halt by the door. 'I saved you . . . Mrs York!'

'Saved? Save the birds, captain!'

Crispin tried to speak, but she slammed the door. He walked back through the meadow and punted across the river to the picket ship, unaware of Quimby's insane moon eyes staring down at him from the rail.

'Crisp . . . What's the matter?' For once the dwarf was gentle. 'What happened?'

Crispin shook his head. He gazed up at the dead bird, struggling to find some solution to the woman's last retort. 'Quimby,' he said in a quiet voice to the dwarf, 'Quimby, she thinks she's a bird.'

During the next week this conviction grew in Crispin's bewildered mind, as did his obsession with the dead bird. Looming over him like an immense murdered angel, the dove's eyes seemed to follow him about the ship, reminding him of when it had first appeared, almost from within his own face, in the mirror-glass of the bridge-house.

It was this sense of identity with the bird that was to spur Crispin to his final stratagem.

Climbing the mast, he secured himself to the lookout's nest, and with a hacksaw cut away the steel cables tangled around the dove's body. In the gathering wind the great white form of the bird swayed and dipped, its fallen wings almost knocking Crispin from his perch. At intervals the rain beat across them, but the drops helped to wash away the blood on the bird's breast and the chips of rust from the hacksaw. At last Crispin lowered the bird to the deck, then lashed it to the hatch cover behind the funnel.

Exhausted, he slept until the next day. At dawn, armed with a machete, he began to eviscerate the bird.

Three days later, Crispin stood on the cliff above the house, the picket ship far below him across the river. The hollow carcass of the dove which he wore over his head and shoulders seemed little heavier than a pillow. In the brief spell of warm sunlight he lifted the outstretched wings, feeling their buoyancy and the cutting flow of air through the feathers. A few stronger gusts moved across the crest of the ridge, almost lifting him into the wind, and he stepped closer to the small oak which hid him from the house below.

Against the trunk rested his rifle and bandoliers. Crispin lowered the wings and gazed up at the sky, making certain for the last time that no stray hawk or peregrine was about. The effectiveness of the disguise had exceeded all his hopes. Kneeling on the ground, the wings furled at his sides and the hollowed head of the bird lowered over his face, he felt he completely resembled the dove.

Below him the ground sloped towards the house. From

the deck of the picket ship the cliff face had seemed almost vertical, but in fact the ground shelved downwards at a steady but gentle gradient. With luck he might even manage to be airborne for a few steps. However, for most of the way to the house he intended simply to run downhill.

As he waited for Catherine York to appear he freed his right arm from the metal clamp he had fastened to the wing bone of the bird. He reached out to set the safety catch on his rifle. By divesting himself of the weapon and his bandoliers, and assuming the disguise of the bird, he had, as he understood, accepted the insane logic of the woman's mind. Yet the symbolic flight he was about to perform would free not only Catherine York, but himself as well, from the spell of the birds.

A door opened in the house, a broken pane of glass catching the sunlight. Crispin stood up behind the oak, his hands bracing themselves on the wings. Catherine York appeared, carrying something across the yard. She paused by the rebuilt nest, her white hair lifting in the breeze, and adjusted some of the feathers.

Stepping from behind the tree, Crispin walked forward down the slope. Ten yards ahead he reached a patch of worn turf. He began to run, the wings flapping unevenly at his sides. As he gained speed his feet raced across the ground. Suddenly the wings steadied as they gained their purchase on the updraught, and he found himself able to glide, the air rushing past his face.

He was a hundred yards from the house when the woman noticed him. A few moments later, when she had brought her shotgun from the kitchen, Crispin was too busy trying to control the speeding glider in which he had become a confused but jubilant passenger. His voice cried out as he soared across the falling ground, feet leaping in ten-yard strides, the smell of the bird's blood and plumage filling his lungs.

He reached the perimeter of the meadow that ringed the house, crossing the hedge fifteen feet above the ground. He was holding with one hand to the soaring carcass of the dove, his head half-lost inside the skull, when the woman fired twice at him. The first charge went through the tail, but the second shot hit him in the chest, down into the soft grass of the meadow among the dead birds.

Half an hour later, when she saw that Crispin had died, Catherine York walked forward to the twisted carcass of the dove and began to pluck away the choicest plumes, carrying them back to the nest which she was building again for the great bird that would come one day and bring back her son.

Noon talk on Millionth Street:

'Sorry, these are the West Millions. You want 9775335th East.'

'Dollar five a cubic foot? Sell!'

'Take a westbound express to 495th Avenue, cross over to a Redline elevator and go up a thousand levels to Plaza Terminal. Carry on south from there and you'll find it between 568th Avenue and 422nd Street.'

'There's a cave-in down at KEN County! Fifty blocks by twenty by thirty levels.'

'Listen to this—"PYROMANIACS STAGE MASS BREAK-OUT! FIRE POLICE CORDON BAY COUNTY!"'

'It's a beautiful counter. Detects up to ·005 per cent monoxide. Cost me three hundred dollars.'

'Have you seen those new intercity sleepers? They take only ten minutes to go up 3,000 levels!'

'Ninety cents a foot? Buy!'

'You say the idea came to you in a dream?' the voice snapped. 'You're sure no one else gave it to you.'

'No,' M. said. A couple of feet away from him a spot-lamp threw a cone of dirty yellow light into his face. He dropped his eyes from the glare and waited as the sergeant paced over to his desk, tapped his fingers on the edge and swung round on him again.

'You talked it over with your friends?'

'Only the first theory,' M. explained. 'About the possibility of flight.'

'But you told me the other theory was more important. Why keep it from them?'

M. hesitated. Outside somewhere a trolley shunted and clanged along the elevated. 'I was afraid they wouldn't understand what I meant.'

The sergeant laughed. 'Do you mean they would have

thought you really were insane?'

M. shifted uncomfortably on the stool. Its seat was only six inches off the floor and his thighs felt like slabs of inflamed rubber. After three hours of cross-questioning logic had faded. 'The concept was a little abstract. There weren't any words for it.'

The sergeant shook his head. 'I'm glad to hear you say it.' He sat down on the desk, watched M. for a moment and then went over to him.

'Now look,' he said confidentially. 'It's getting late. Do you still think both theories are reasonable?'

M. looked up. 'Aren't they?'

The sergeant turned to the man watching in the shadows by the window. 'We're wasting our time,' he snapped. 'I'll hand him over to Psycho. You've seen enough, haven't you, Doctor?'

The surgeon stared at his hands. He had taken no part in the interrogation, as if bored by the sergeant's method of approach.

'There's something I want to find out,' he said. 'Leave me alone with him for half an hour.'

When the sergeant had gone the surgeon sat down behind the desk and stared out of the window, listening to the dull hum of air through the ventilator shaft which rose out of the street below the station. A few roof lights were still burning and two hundred yards away a single policeman patrolled the iron catwalk running above the street, his boots ringing across the darkness.

M. sat on the stool, elbows between his knees, trying to edge a little life back into his legs.

Eventually the surgeon glanced down at the charge sheet.

Name........................ Franz M.
Age.......................... 20.
Occupation................. Student.

Address..........................3599719 West 783rd St, Level
                               549–7705–45 KNI (Local).
Charge........................ Vagrancy.

'Tell me about this dream,' he said, idly flexing a steel
rule between his hands as he looked across at M.

'I think you've heard everything, sir,' M. said.

'In detail.'

M. shifted uneasily. 'There wasn't much to it, and
what I do remember isn't too clear now.'

The surgeon yawned. M. waited and then started to
recite what he had already repeated twenty times.

'I was suspended in the air above a flat stretch of open
ground, something like the floor of an enormous arena.
My arms were out at my sides, and I was looking down,
floating——'

'Hold on,' the surgeon interrupted. 'Are you sure you
weren't swimming?'

'No,' M. said. 'I'm certain I wasn't. All around me
there was free space. That was the most important part
about it. There were no walls. Nothing but emptiness.
That's all I remember.'

The surgeon ran his finger along the edge of the rule.

'Go on.'

'Well, the dream gave me the idea of building a flying
machine. One of my friends helped me construct it.'

The surgeon nodded. Almost absently he picked up the
charge sheet and crushed it with a single motion of his
hand.

'Don't be absurd, Franz!' Gregson remonstrated. They
took their places in the chemistry cafeteria queue. 'It's
against the laws of hydrodynamics. Where would you
get your buoyancy?'

'Suppose you had a rigid fabric vane,' Franz explained
as they shuffled past the hatchways. 'Say ten feet across,

like one of those composition wall sections, with hand grips on the ventral surface. And then you jumped down from the gallery at the Coliseum Stadium. What would happen?'

'You'd make a hole in the floor. Why?'

'No, seriously.'

'If it was large enough and held together you'd swoop down like a paper dart.'

'Glide,' Franz said. 'Right.' Thirty levels above them one of the intercity expresses roared over, rattling the tables and cutlery in the cafeteria. Franz waited until they reached a table and sat forward, his food forgotten.

'And say you attached a propulsive unit, such as a battery-driven ventilator fan, or one of those rockets they use on the Sleepers. With enough thrust to overcome your weight. What then?'

Gregson shrugged. 'If you could control the thing, you'd, you'd ...' He frowned at Franz. 'What's the word? You're always using it.'

'Fly.'

'Basically, Matheson, the machine is simple,' Sanger, the physics lector, commented as they entered the science library. 'An elementary application of the Venturi Principle. But what's the point of it? A trapeze would serve its purpose equally well, and be far less dangerous. In the first place consider the enormous clearances it would require. I hardly think the traffic authorities will look upon it with any favour.'

'I know it wouldn't be practical here,' Franz admitted. 'But in a large open area it should be.'

'Allowed. I suggest you immediately negotiate with the Arena Garden on Level 347–25,' the lector said whimsically. 'I'm sure they'll be glad to hear about your scheme.'

Franz smiled politely. 'That wouldn't be large enough.

I was really thinking of an area of totally free space. In three dimensions, as it were.'

Sanger looked at Franz curiously. 'Free space? Isn't that a contradiction in terms? Space is a dollar a cubic foot.' He scratched his nose. 'Have you begun to construct this machine yet?'

'No,' Franz said.

'In that event I should try to forget all about it. Remember, Matheson, the task of science is to consolidate existing knowledge, to systematize and reinterpret the discoveries of the past, not to chase wild dreams into the future.'

He nodded and disappeared among the dusty shelves.

Gregson was waiting on the steps.

'Well?' he asked.

'Let's try it out this afternoon,' Franz said. 'We'll cut Text 5 Pharmacology. I know those Fleming readings backwards. I'll ask Dr McGhee for a couple of passes.'

They left the library and walked down the narrow, dimly-lit alley which ran behind the huge new civil engineering laboratories. Over seventy-five per cent of the student enrolment was in the architectural and engineering faculties, a meagre two per cent in pure sciences. Consequently the physics and chemistry libraries were housed in the oldest quarter of the university, in two virtually condemned galvanized hutments which once contained the now closed philosophy school.

At the end of the alley they entered the university plaza and started to climb the iron stairway leading to the next level a hundred feet above. Halfway up a white-helmeted F.P. checked them cursorily with his detector and waved them past.

'What did Sanger think?' Gregson asked as they stepped up into 637th Street and walked across to the suburban elevator station.

'He's no use at all,' Franz said. 'He didn't even begin to understand what I was talking about.'

Gregson laughed ruefully. 'I don't know whether I do.'

Franz took a ticket from the automat and mounted the down platform. An elevator dropped slowly towards him, its bell jangling.

'Wait until this afternoon,' he called back. 'You're really going to see something.'

The floor manager at the Coliseum initialled the two passes.

'Students, eh? All right.' He jerked a thumb at the long package Franz and Gregson were carrying. 'What have you got there?'

'It's a device for measuring air velocities,' Franz told him.

The manager grunted and released the stile.

Out in the centre of the empty arena Franz undid the package and they assembled the model. It had a broad fan-like wing of wire and paper, a narrow strutted fuselage and a high curving tail.

Franz picked it up and launched it into the air. The model glided for twenty feet and then slithered to a stop across the sawdust.

'Seems to be stable,' Franz said. 'We'll tow it first.'

He pulled a reel of twine from his pocket and tied one end to the nose. As they ran forward the model lifted gracefully into the air and followed them around the stadium, ten feet off the floor.

'Let's try the rockets now,' Franz said. He adjusted the wing and tail settings and fitted three firework display rockets into a wire bracket mounted above the wing.

The stadium was four hundred feet in diameter and had a roof two hundred and fifty feet high. They carried the model over to one side and Franz lit the tapers.

There was a burst of flame and the model accelerated across the floor, two feet in the air, a bright trail of coloured smoke spitting out behind it. Its wings rocked gently from side to side. Suddenly the tail burst into flames. The model lifted steeply and looped up towards the roof, stalled just before it hit one of the pilot lights and dived down into the sawdust.

They ran across to it and stamped out the glowing cinders. 'Franz!' Gregson shouted. 'It's incredible! It actually works.'

Franz kicked the shattered fuselage. 'Of course it works,' he said impatiently. 'But as Sanger said, what's the point of it?'

'The point? It flies! Isn't that enough?'

'No. I want one big enough to hold me.'

'Franz, slow down. Be reasonable. Where could you fly it?'

'I don't know,' Franz said fiercely. 'But there must be somewhere!'

The floor manager and two assistants, carrying fire extinguishers, ran across the stadium to them.

'Did you hide the matches?' Franz asked quickly. 'They'll lynch us if they think we're Pyros.'

Three afternoons later Franz took the elevator up 150 levels to 677–98, where the Precinct Estate Office had its bureau.

'There's a big development between 493 and 554 in the next sector,' one of the clerks told him. 'I don't know whether that's any good to you. Sixty blocks by twenty by fifteen levels.'

'Nothing bigger?' Franz queried.

The clerk looked up. 'Bigger? No. *What* are you looking for—a slight case of agoraphobia?'

Franz straightened the maps spread across the counter. 'I wanted to find an area of more or less continuous development. Two or three hundred blocks long.'

The clerk shook his head and went back to his ledger. 'Didn't you go to engineering school?' he asked scornfully. 'The City won't take it. One hundred blocks is the maximum.'

Franz thanked him and left.

A south-bound express took him to the development in two hours. He left the car at the detour point and walked the three hundred yards to the end of the level.

The street, a seedy but busy thoroughfare of garment shops and small business premises running through the huge ten-mile-thick B.I.R. Industrial Cube, ended abruptly in a tangle of ripped girders and concrete. A steel rail had been erected along the edge and Franz looked down over it into the cavity, three miles long, a mile wide and twelve hundred feet deep, which thousands of engineers and demolition workers were tearing out of the matrix of the City.

Eight hundred feet below him unending lines of trucks and railcars carried away the rubble and debris, and clouds of dust swirled up into the arc-lights blazing down from the roof. As he watched, a chain of explosions ripped along the wall on his left and the whole face slipped and fell slowly towards the floor, revealing a perfect cross-section through fifteen levels of the City.

Franz had seen big developments before, and his own parents had died in the historic QUA County cave-in ten years earlier, when three master-pillars had sheared and two hundred levels of the City had abruptly sunk ten thousand feet, squashing half a million people like flies in a concertina, but the enormous gulf of emptiness still stunned his imagination.

All around him, standing and sitting on the jutting terraces of girders, a silent throng stared down.

'They say they're going to build gardens and parks for us,' an elderly man at Franz's elbow remarked in a patient voice. 'I even heard they might be able to get a tree. It'll be the only tree in the whole county.'

A man in a frayed sweat-shirt spat over the rail. 'That's what they always say. At a dollar a foot promises are all they can waste space on.'

Below them a woman who had been looking out into the air started to simper nervously. Two bystanders took her by the arms and tried to lead her away. The woman began to thresh about and an F.P. came over and pulled her away roughly.

'Poor fool,' the man in the sweat-shirt commented. 'She probably lived out there somewhere. They gave her ninety cents a foot when they took it away from her. She doesn't know yet she'll have to pay a dollar ten to get it back. Now they're going to start charging five cents an hour just to sit up here and watch.'

Franz looked out over the railing for a couple of hours and then bought a postcard from one of the vendors and walked back to the elevator.

He called in to see Gregson before returning to the student dormitory. The Gregsons lived in the West millions on 985th Avenue, in a top three-room flat right under the roof. Franz had known them since his parents' death, but Gregson's mother still regarded him with a mixture of sympathy and suspicion. As she let him in with her customary smile of welcome he noticed her glancing at the detector mounted in the hall.

Gregson was in his room, happily cutting out frames of paper and pasting them on to a great rickety construction that vaguely resembled Franz's model.

'Hullo, Franz. What was it like?'

Franz shrugged. 'Just a development. Worth seeing.'

Gregson pointed to his construction. 'Do you think we can try it out there?'

'We could do.' Franz sat down on the bed. He picked up a paper dart lying beside him and tossed it out of the window. It swam into the street, lazed down in a wide spiral and vanished into the open mouth of the ventilator shaft.

'When are you going to build another model?' Gregson asked.

'I'm not.'

Gregson looked up. 'Why? You've proved your theory.'

'That's not what I'm after.'

'I don't get you, Franz. What are you after?'

'Free space.'

'Free?' Gregson repeated.

Franz nodded. 'In both senses.'

Gregson shook his head sadly and snipped out another paper panel. 'Franz, you're mad.'

Franz stood up. 'Take this room,' he said. 'It's twenty feet by fifteen by ten. Extend its dimensions infinitely. What do you find?'

'A development.'

'*Infinitely!*'

'Non-functional space.'

'Well?' Franz asked patiently.

'The concept's absurd.'

'Why?'

'Because it couldn't exist.'

Franz pounded his forehead in despair. '*Why* couldn't it?'

Gregson gestured with the scissors. 'It's self-contradictory. Like the statement "I am lying". Just a verbal freak. Interesting theoretically, but it's pointless to press it for meaning.' He tossed the scissors on to the table. 'And anyway, do you know how much free space would cost?'

Franz went over to the bookshelf and pulled out one of the volumes. 'Let's have a look at your street atlas.' He turned to the index. 'This gives a thousand levels. KNI

County, one hundred thousand cubic miles, population 30 million.'

Gregson nodded.

Franz closed the atlas. 'Two hundred and fifty counties, including KNI, together form the 493rd Sector, and an association of 1,500 adjacent sectors comprise the 298th Local Union.' He broke off and looked at Gregson. 'As a matter of interest, ever heard of it?'

Gregson shook his head. 'No. How did——'

Franz slapped the atlas on to the table. 'Roughly 4×10^{15} cubic Great-Miles.' He leaned on the window-ledge. 'Now tell me: what lies beyond the 298th Local Union?'

'Other unions, I suppose,' Gregson said. 'I don't see your difficulty.'

'And beyond those?'

'Farther ones. Why not?'

'For ever?' Franz pressed.

'Well, as far as for ever is.'

'The great street directory in the old Treasury Library on 247th Street is the largest in the county,' Franz said. 'I went down there this morning. It occupies three complete levels. Millions of volumes. But it doesn't extend beyond the 598th Local Union. No one there had any idea what lay farther out. Why not?'

'Why should they?' Gregson asked. 'Franz, what are you driving at?'

Franz walked across to the door. 'Come down to the Bio-History Museum. I'll show you.'

The birds perched on humps of rock or waddled about the sandy paths between the water pools.

' "Archaeopteryx",' Franz read off one of the cage indicators. The bird, lean and mildewed, uttered a painful croak when he fed a handful of beans to it.

'Some of these birds have the remnants of a pectoral

41

girdle,' Franz said. 'Minute fragments of bone embedded in the tissues around their rib cages.'

'Wings?'

'Dr McGhee thinks so.'

They walked out between the lines of cages.

'When does he think they were flying?'

'Before the Foundation,' Franz said. 'Three million years ago.'

When they were outside the museum they started down 859th Avenue. Halfway down the street a dense crowd had gathered and people were packed into the windows and balconies above the elevated, watching a squad of Fire Police break their way into a house.

The bulkheads at either end of the block had been closed and heavy steel traps sealed off the stairways from the levels above and below. The ventilator and exhaust shafts were silent and already the air was stale and soupy.

'Pyros,' Gregson murmured. 'We should have brought our masks.'

'It's only a scare,' Franz said. He pointed to the monoxide detectors which were out everywhere, their long snouts sucking at the air. The dial needles stood safely at zero. 'Let's wait in the restaurant opposite.'

They edged their way over to the restaurant, sat down in the window and ordered coffee. This, like everything else on the menu, was cold. All cooking appliances were thermostated to a maximum 95°F., and only in the more expensive restaurants and hotels was it possible to obtain food that was at most tepid.

Below them in the street a lot of shouting went up. The Fire Police seemed unable to penetrate beyond the ground floor of the house and had started to baton back the crowd. An electric winch was wheeled up and bolted to the girders running below the kerb, and half a dozen heavy steel grabs were carried into the house and hooked round the walls.

Gregson laughed. 'The owners are going to be surprised when they get home.'

Franz was watching the house. It was a narrow shabby dwelling sandwiched between a large wholesale furniture store and a new supermarket. An old sign running across the front had been painted over and evidently the ownership had recently changed. The present tenants had made a half-hearted attempt to convert the ground floor room into a cheap stand-up diner. The Fire Police appeared to be doing their best to wreck everything, and pies and smashed crockery were strewn all over the pavement.

The noise died away and everyone waited as the winch began to revolve. The hawsers wound in and tautened, and the front wall of the house staggered outwards in rigid jerky movements.

Suddenly there was a yell from the crowd.

Franz raised his arm. 'Up there! Look!'

On the fourth floor a man and woman had come to the window and were looking down helplessly. The man lifted the woman on to the ledge and she crawled out and clung to one of the waste pipes. Bottles were lobbed up at them and bounced down among the police. A wide crack split the house from top to bottom and the floor on which the man was standing dropped and catapulted him backwards out of sight. Then one of the lintels in the first floor snapped and the entire house tipped over and collapsed.

Franz and Gregson stood up, almost knocking over the table.

The crowd surged forward through the cordon. When the dust had settled there was nothing left but a heap of masonry and twisted beams. Embedded in this was the battered figure of the man. Almost smothered by the dust he moved slowly, trying to free himself with one hand, and the crowd started roaring again as one of the grabs wound in and dragged him down under the rubble.

The manager of the restaurant pushed past Franz and leant out of the window, his eyes fixed on the dial of a portable detector. Its needle, like all the others, pointed to zero.

A dozen hoses were playing on the remains of the house and after a few minutes the crowd shifted and began to thin out.

The manager switched off the detector and left the window, nodding to Franz. 'Damn Pyros. You can relax now, boys.'

Franz pointed at the detector. 'Your dial was dead. There wasn't a trace of monoxide anywhere here. How do you know they were Pyros?'

'Don't worry, we know.' He smiled obliquely. 'We don't want that sort of element in this neighbourhood.'

Franz shrugged and sat down. 'I suppose that's one way of getting rid of them.'

The manager eyed Franz. 'That's right, boy. This is a good dollar five neighbourhood.' He smirked to himself. 'Maybe a dollar six now everybody knows about our safety record.'

'Careful, Franz,' Gregson warned him when the manager had gone. 'He may be right. Pyromaniacs do take over small cafes and food bars.'

Franz stirred his coffee. 'Dr McGhee estimates that at least fifteen per cent of the City's population are submerged Pyros. He's convinced the number's growing and that eventually the whole City will flame-out.'

He pushed away his coffee. 'How much money have you got?'

'On me?'

'Altogether.'

'About thirty dollars.'

'I've saved fifteen,' Franz said. 'Forty-five dollars; that

should be enough for three or four weeks.'

'Where?' Gregson asked.

'On a Supersleeper.'

'Super——!' Gregson broke off, alarmed. 'Three or four weeks! What do you mean?'

'There's only one way to find out,' Franz explained calmly. 'I can't just sit here thinking. Somewhere there's free space and I'll ride the Sleeper until I find it. Will you lend me your thirty dollars?'

'But Franz——'

'If I don't find anything within a couple of weeks I'll change tracks and come back.'

'But the ticket will cost...' Gregson searched '... billions. Forty-five dollars won't even get you out of the Sector.'

'That's just for coffee and sandwiches,' Franz said. 'The ticket will be free.' He looked up from the table. 'You know...'

Gregson shook his head doubtfully. 'Can you try that on the Supersleepers?'

'Why not? If they query it I'll say I'm going back the long way round. Greg, will you?'

'I don't know if I should.' Gregson played helplessly with his coffee. 'Franz, how can there be free space? How?'

'That's what I'm going to find out,' Franz said. 'Think of it as my first physics practical.'

Passenger distances on the transport system were measured point to point by the application of $a = \sqrt{b^2 + c^2 + d^2}$. The actual itinerary taken was the passenger's responsibility, and as long as he remained within the system he could choose any route he liked. Tickets were checked only at the station exits, where necessary surcharges were collected by an inspector. If the passenger was unable to pay the surcharge—ten cents a mile—he was sent back to his original destination.

Franz and Gregson entered the station on 984th Street and went over to the large console where tickets were automatically dispensed. Franz put in a penny and pressed the destination button marked 984. The machine rumbled, coughed out a ticket, and the change slot gave him back his coin.

'Well, Greg, goodbye,' Franz said as they moved towards the barrier. 'I'll see you in about two weeks. They're covering me down at the dormitory. Tell Sanger I'm on Fire Duty.'

'What if you don't get back, Franz?' Gregson asked. 'Suppose they take you off the Sleeper?'

'How can they? I've got my ticket.'

'And if you do find free space? Will you come back then?'

'If I can.'

Franz patted Gregson on the shoulder reassuringly, waved and disappeared among the commuters.

He took the local Suburban Green to the district junction in the next county. The Green Line train travelled at an interrupted 70 m.p.h. and the ride took two and a half hours.

At the junction he changed to an express elevator which lifted him out of the sector in ninety minutes, at 400 m.p.h. Another fifty minutes in a Through-Sector Special brought him to the Mainline Terminus which served the Union.

There he bought a coffee and gathered his determination together. Supersleepers ran east and west, halting at this and every tenth station. The next arrived in seventy-two hours time, westbound.

The Mainline Terminus was the largest station Franz had seen, a mile-long cavern thirty levels in depth. Hundreds of elevator shafts sank through the station and the maze of platforms, escalators, restaurants, hotels and theatres seemed like an exaggerated replica of the City itself.

Getting his bearings from one of the information booths, Franz made his way up an escalator to Tier 15, where the Supersleepers berthed. Running the length of the station were two steel vacuum tunnels each three hundred feet in diameter, supported at thirty-four intervals by huge concrete buttresses.

Franz walked along the platform and stopped by the telescopic gangway that plunged into one of the airlocks. Two hundred and seventy degrees true, he thought, gazing up at the curving underbelly of the tunnel. It must come out somewhere. He had forty-five dollars in his pocket, sufficient coffee and sandwich money to last him three weeks, six if he needed it, time anyway to find the City's end.

He passed the next three days nursing cups of coffee in any of the thirty cafeterias in the station, reading discarded newspapers and sleeping in the local Red trains which ran four-hour journeys round the nearest sector.

When at last the Supersleeper came in he joined the small group of Fire Police and municipal officials waiting by the gangway, and followed them into the train. There were two cars; a sleeper which no one used, and a day coach.

Franz took an inconspicuous corner seat near one of the indicator panels in the day coach, and pulled out his notebook ready to make his first entry.

1st Day : West 270°. Union 4,350.

'Coming out for a drink?' a Fire Captain across the aisle asked. 'We have a ten-minute break here.'

'No thanks,' Franz said. 'I'll hold your seat for you.'

Dollar five a cubic foot. Free space, he knew, would bring the price down. There was no need to leave the train or make too many inquiries. All he had to do was borrow a paper and watch the market averages.

2nd Day: West 270°. Union 7,550.

'They're slowly cutting down on these Sleepers,' someone told him. 'Everyone sits in the day coach. Look at this one. Seats sixty, and only four people in it. There's no need to move around. People are staying where they are. In a few years there'll be nothing left but the suburban services.'

97 cents.

At an average of a dollar a cubic foot, Franz calculated idly, it's so far worth about 4×10^{27}.

'Going on to the next stop, are you? Well, goodbye young fellow.'

Few of the passengers stayed on the Sleeper for more than three or four hours. By the end of the second day Franz's back and neck ached from the constant acceleration. He managed to take a little exercise walking up and down the narrow corridor in the deserted sleeping coach, but had to spend most of his time strapped to his seat as the train began its long braking runs into the next station.

3rd Day: West 270°. Federation 657.

'Interesting, but how could you demonstrate it?'

'It's just an odd idea of mine,' Franz said, screwing up the sketch and dropping it in the disposal chute. 'Hasn't any real application.'

'Curious, but it rings a bell somewhere.'

Franz sat up. 'Do you mean you've seen machines like this? In a newspaper or a book?'

'No, no. In a dream.'

Every half day's run the pilot signed the log, the crew

handed over to their opposites on an Eastbound sleeper, crossed the platform and started back for home.

125 cents.

8×10^{33}.

4th Day: West 270°. Federation 1,225.

'Dollar a cubic foot. You in the estate business?'

'Starting up,' Franz said easily. 'I'm hoping to open a new office of my own.'

He played cards, bought coffee and rolls from the dispenser in the washroom, watched the indicator panel and listened to the talk around him.

'Believe me, a time will come when each union, each sector, almost I might say, each street and avenue will have achieved complete local independence. Equipped with its own power services, aerators, reservoirs, farm laboratories . . .'

The car bore.

6×10^{75}.

5th Day: West 270°. 17th Greater Federation.

At a kiosk on the station Franz bought a clip of razor blades and glanced at the brochure put out by the local chamber of commerce.

'12,000 levels, 98 cents a foot, unique Elm Drive, fire safety records unequalled . . .'

He went back to the train, shaved, and counted the thirty dollars left. He was now ninety-five million Great-Miles from the suburban station on 984th Street and he knew he could not delay his return much longer. Next time he would save up a couple of thousand.

7×10^{127}.

7th Day: West 270°. 212th Metropolitan Empire.

Franz peered at the indicator.

'Aren't we stopping here?' he asked a man three seats away. 'I wanted to find out the market average.'

'Varies. Anything from fifty cents a——'

'Fifty!' Franz shot back, jumping up. 'When's the next stop? I've got to get off!'

'Not here, son.' He put out a restraining hand. 'This is Night Town. You in real estate?'

Franz nodded, holding himself back. 'I thought ...'

'Relax.' He came and sat opposite Franz. 'It's just one big slum. Dead areas. In places it goes as low as five cents. There are no services, no power.'

It took them two days to pass through.

'City Authority are starting to seal it off,' the man told him. 'Huge blocks. It's the only thing they can do. What happens to the people inside I hate to think.' He chewed on a sandwich. 'Strange, but there are a lot of these black areas. You don't hear about them, but they're growing. Starts in a back street in some ordinary dollar neighbourhood; a bottleneck in the sewage disposal system, not enough ash cans, and before you know it—a million cubic miles have gone back to jungle. They try a relief scheme, pump in a little cyanide, and then—brick it up. Once they do that they're closed for good.'

Franz nodded, listening to the dull humming air.

'Eventually there'll be nothing left but these black areas. The City will be one huge cemetery!'

10th Day: East 90°. 755th Greater Metropolitan——

'Wait!' Franz leapt out of his seat and stared at the indicator panel.

'What's the matter?' someone opposite asked.

'East!' Franz shouted. He banged the panel sharply with his hand but the lights held. 'Has this train changed direction?'

'No, it's eastbound,' another of the passengers told him. 'Are you on the wrong train?'

'It should be heading west,' Franz insisted. 'It has been for the last ten days.'

'Ten days!' the man exclaimed. 'Have you been on this sleeper for ten days?'

Franz went forward and found the car attendant. 'Which way is this train going? West?'

The attendant shook his head. 'East, sir. It's always been going east.'

'You're crazy,' Franz snapped. 'I want to see the pilot's log.'

'I'm afraid that isn't possible. May I see your ticket, sir?'

'Listen,' Franz said weakly, all the accumulated frustration of the last twenty years mounting inside him. 'I've been on this . . .'

He stopped and went back to his seat.

The five other passengers watched him carefully.

'Ten days,' one of them was still repeating in an awed voice.

Two minutes later someone came and asked Franz for his ticket.

'And of course it was completely in order,' the police surgeon commented. 'Strangely enough there's no regulation to prevent anyone else doing the same thing. I used to go for free rides myself when I was younger, though I never tried anything like your journey.'

He went back to the desk. 'We'll drop the charge,' he said. 'You're not a vagrant in any indictable sense, and the transport authorities can do nothing against you. How this curvature was built into the system they can't explain, it seems to be some inherent feature of the City itself. Now about yourself. Are you going to continue this search?'

'I want to build a flying machine,' M. said carefully. 'There must be free space somewhere. I don't know . . . perhaps on the lower levels.'

The surgeon stood up. 'I'll see the sergeant and get him to hand you over to one of our psychiatrists. He'll be able to help you with your dreams!'

The surgeon hesitated before opening the door. 'Look,' he began to explain, 'you can't get out of time, can you? Subjectively it's a plastic dimension, but whatever you do to yourself you'll never be able to stop that clock'— he pointed to the one on the desk—'or make it run backwards. In exactly the same way you can't get out of the City.'

'The analogy doesn't hold,' M. said. He gestured at the walls around them and the lights in the street outside. 'All this was built by us. The question nobody can answer is: what was here before we built it?'

'It's always been here,' the surgeon said. 'Not these particular bricks and girders, but others before them. You accept that time has no beginning and no end. The City is as old as time and continuous with it.'

'The first bricks were laid by someone,' M. insisted. 'There was the Foundation.'

'A myth. Only the scientists believe in that, and even they don't try to make too much of it. Most of them privately admit that the Foundation Stone is nothing more than a superstition. We pay it lip service out of convenience, and because it gives us a sense of tradition. Obviously there can't have been a first brick. If there was, how can you explain who laid it and, even more difficult, where they came from?'

'There must be free space somewhere,' M. said doggedly. 'The City must have bounds.'

'Why?' the surgeon asked. 'It can't be floating in the middle of nowhere. Or is that what you're trying to believe?'

M. sank back limply. 'No.'

The surgeon watched M. silently for a few minutes and paced back to the desk. 'This peculiar fixation of yours puzzles me. You're caught between what the psychiatrists call paradoxical faces. I suppose you haven't misinterpreted something you've heard about the Wall?'

M. looked up. 'Which wall?'

The surgeon nodded to himself. 'Some advanced opinion maintains that there's a wall around the City, through which it's impossible to penetrate. I don't pretend to understand the theory myself. It's far too abstract and sophisticated. Anyway I suspect they've confused this Wall with the bricked-up black areas you passed through on the Sleeper. I prefer the accepted view that the City stretches out in all directions without limits.'

He went over to the door. 'Wait here, and I'll see about getting you a probationary release. Don't worry, the psychiatrists will straighten everything out for you.'

When the surgeon had left M. stared at the floor, too exhausted to feel relieved. He stood up and stretched himself, walking unsteadily round the room.

Outside the last pilot lights were going out and the patrolman on the catwalk under the roof was using his torch. A police car roared down one of the avenues crossing the street, its rails screaming. Three lights snapped on along the street and then one by one went off again.

M. wondered why Gregson hadn't come down to the station. Then the calendar on the desk riveted his attention. The date exposed on the fly leaf was 12 August. That was the day he had started off on his journey— exactly three weeks ago.

Today!

Take a westbound Green to 298th Street, cross over at the intersection and get a Red elevator up to Level 237. Walk down to the station on Route 175, change to a 438 suburban and go down to 795th Street. Take a Blue line to the Plaza, get off at 4th and 275th, turn left at the roundabout and——

You're back where you first started from.

$Hell \times 10^n$.

'The signs, Doctor! Have you seen the signs?'

Frowning with annoyance, Dr Franklin quickened his pace and hurried down the hospital steps towards the line of parked cars. Over his shoulder he caught a glimpse of a young man in ragged sandals and paint-stained jeans waving to him from the far side of the drive.

'Dr Franklin! The signs!'

Head down, Franklin swerved around an elderly couple approaching the out-patients department. His car was over a hundred yards away. Too tired to start running himself, he waited for the young man to catch him up.

'All right, Hathaway, what is it this time?' he snapped. 'I'm sick of you hanging around here all day.'

Hathaway lurched to a halt in front of him, uncut black hair like an awning over his eyes. He brushed it back with a claw-like hand and turned on a wild smile, obviously glad to see Franklin and oblivious of the latter's hostility.

'I've been trying to reach you at night, Doctor, but your wife always puts the phone down on me,' he explained without a hint of rancour, as if well-used to this kind of snub. 'And I didn't want to look for you inside the Clinic.' They were standing by a privet hedge that shielded them from the lower windows of the main administrative block, but Franklin's regular rendezvous with Hathaway and his strange messianic cries had already become the subject of amused comment.

Franklin began to say: 'I appreciate that——' but Hathaway brushed this aside. 'Forget it, Doctor, there are more important things now. They've started to build the first big signs! Over a hundred feet high, on the traffic islands outside town. They'll soon have all the approach roads covered. When they do we might as well stop thinking.'

'Your trouble is that you're thinking too much,' Franklin told him. 'You've been rambling about these signs for weeks now. Tell me, have you actually seen one signalling?'

Hathaway tore a handful of leaves from the hedge, exasperated by this irrelevancy. 'Of course I haven't, that's the whole point, Doctor.' He dropped his voice as a group of nurses walked past, watching his raffish figure out of the corners of their eyes. 'The construction gangs were out again last night, laying huge power cables. You'll see them on the way home. Everything's nearly ready now.'

'They're traffic signs,' Franklin explained patiently. 'The flyover has just been completed. Hathaway, for God's sake, relax. Try to think of Dora and the child.'

'I *am* thinking of them!' Hathaway's voice rose to a controlled scream. 'Those cables were 40,000-volt lines, Doctor, with terrific switch-gear. The trucks were loaded with enormous metal scaffolds. Tomorrow they'll start lifting them up all over the city, they'll block off half the sky! What do you think Dora will be like after six months of that? We've got to stop them, Doctor, they're trying to transistorize our brains!'

Embarrassed by Hathaway's high-pitched shouting, Franklin had momentarily lost his sense of direction. Helplessly he searched the sea of cars for his own. 'Hathaway, I can't waste any more time talking to you. Believe me, you need skilled help, these obsessions are beginning to master you.'

Hathaway started to protest, and Franklin raised his right hand firmly. 'Listen. For the last time, if you can show me one of these signs, and prove it's transmitting subliminal commands, I'll go to the police with you But you haven't got a shred of evidence, and you know it. Subliminal advertising was banned thirty years ago, and the laws have never been repealed. Anyway, the technique was unsatisfactory, any success it had was marginal. Your idea of a huge conspiracy with all these thousands of giant signs everywhere is preposterous.'

'All right, Doctor.' Hathaway leaned against the bonnet of one of the cars. His mood seemed to switch abruptly from one level to the next. He watched Franklin amiably. 'What's the matter—lost your car?'

'All your damned shouting has confused me.' Franklin pulled out his ignition key and read the number off the tag: 'NYN 299-566-367-21—can you see it?'

Hathaway leaned around lazily, one sandal up on the bonnet, surveying the square of a thousand or so cars facing them. 'Difficult, isn't it, when they're all identical, even the same colour? Thirty years ago there were about ten different makes, each in a dozen colours.'

Franklin spotted his car and began to walk towards it. 'Sixty years ago there were a hundred makes. What of it? The economies of standardization are obviously bought at a price.'

Hathaway drummed his palm on the roofs. 'But these cars aren't all that cheap, Doctor. In fact, comparing them on an average income basis with those of thirty years ago they're about forty per cent more expensive. With only one make being produced you'd expect a substantial reduction in price, not an increase.'

'Maybe,' Franklin said, opening his door. 'But mechanically the cars of today are far more sophisticated. They're lighter, more durable, safer to drive.'

Hathaway shook his head sceptically. 'They *bore* me. The same model, same styling, same colour, year after year. It's a sort of communism.' He rubbed a greasy finger over the windshield. 'This is a new one again, isn't it, Doctor? Where's the old one—you only had it for three months?'

'I traded it in,' Franklin told him, starting the engine. 'If you ever had any money you'd realize that it's the most economical way of owning a car. You don't keep driving the same one until it falls apart. It's the same with everything else—television sets, washing machines, refrigerators. But you aren't faced with the problem.'

Hathway ignored the gibe, and leaned his elbow on Franklin's window. 'Not a bad idea, either, Doctor. It gives me time to think. I'm not working a twelve-hour day to pay for a lot of things I'm too busy to use before they're obsolete.'

He waved as Franklin reversed the car out of its line, then shouted into the wake of exhaust: 'Drive with your eyes closed, Doctor!'

On the way home Franklin kept carefully to the slowest of the four-speed lanes. As usual after his discussions with Hathaway, he felt vaguely depressed. He realized that unconsciously he envied Hathaway his footloose existence. Despite the grimy cold-water apartment in the shadow and roar of the flyover, despite his nagging wife and their sick child, and the endless altercations with the landlord and the supermarket credit manager, Hathaway still retained his freedom intact. Spared any responsibilities, he could resist the smallest encroachment upon him by the rest of society, if only by generating obsessive fantasies such as his latest one about subliminal advertising.

The ability to react to stimuli, even irrationally, was a valid criterion of freedom. By contrast, what freedom Franklin possessed was peripheral, sharply demarked by the manifold responsibilities in the centre of his life—the three mortgages on his home, the mandatory rounds of cocktail parties, the private consultancy occupying most of Saturday which paid the instalments on the multitude of household gadgets, clothes and past holidays. About the only time he had to himself was driving to and from work.

But at least the roads were magnificent. Whatever other criticisms might be levelled at the present society, it certainly knew how to build roads. Eight-, ten- and twelve-lane expressways interlaced across the country, plunging from overhead causeways into the giant car parks in the centre of the cities, or dividing into the great suburban arteries with their multi-acre parking aprons around the marketing centres. Together the roadways and car parks covered more than a third of the country's entire area, and in the neighbourhood of the cities the proportion was higher. The old cities were surrounded by the vast motion sculptures of the clover-leaves and flyovers, but even so the congestion was unremitting.

The ten-mile journey to his home in fact covered over twenty-five miles and took him twice as long as it had done before the construction of the expressway, the additional miles contained within the three giant clover-leaves. New cities were springing from the motels, cafés and car marts around the highways. At the slightest hint of an intersection a shanty town of shacks and filling stations sprawled away among the forest of electric signs and route indicators.

All around him cars bulleted along, streaming towards the suburbs. Relaxed by the smooth motion of the car, Franklin edged outwards into the next speed-lane. As he accelerated from 40 to 50 m.p.h. a strident ear-jarring noise drummed out from his tyres, shaking the chassis of the car. Ostensibly an aid to lane discipline, the surface of the road was covered with a mesh of small rubber studs, spaced progressively farther apart in each of the lanes so that the tyre hum resonated exactly on 40, 50, 60 and 70 m.p.h. Driving at an intermediate speed for more than a few seconds became nervously exhausting, and soon resulted in damage to the car and tyres.

When the studs wore out they were replaced by slightly different patterns, matching those on the latest tyres, so that regular tyre changes were necessary, increasing the safety and efficiency of the expressway. It also increased the revenues of the car and tyre manufacturers. Most cars over six months old soon fell to pieces under the steady battering, but this was regarded as a desirable end, the greater turnover reducing the unit price and making more frequent model changes, as well as ridding the roads of dangerous vehicles.

A quarter of a mile ahead, at the approach to the first of the clover-leaves, the traffic stream was slowing, huge police signs signalling 'Lanes Closed Ahead' and 'Drop Speed by 10 m.p.h.'. Franklin tried to return to the previous lane, but the cars were jammed bumper to bumper. As the chassis began to shudder and vibrate, jarring his spine, he clamped his teeth and tried to restrain himself from sounding the horn. Other drivers were less self-controlled and everywhere engines were plunging and snarling, horns blaring. Road taxes were now so high, up to thirty per cent of the gross national product (by contrast, income taxes were a bare two per cent) that any delay on the expressways called for an immediate government inquiry, and the major departments of state were concerned with the administration of the road systems.

Nearer the clover-leaf the lanes had been closed to allow a gang of construction workers to erect a massive metal sign on one of the traffic islands. The palisaded area swarmed with engineers and surveyors, and Franklin assumed that this was the sign Hathaway had seen unloaded the previous night. His apartment was in one of the gimcrack buildings in the settlement that straggled away around a near-by flyover, a low-rent area inhabited by service-station personnel, waitresses and other migrant labour.

The sign was enormous, at least a hundred feet high, fitted with heavy concave grilles similar to radar bowls. Rooted in a series of concrete caissons, it reared high into the air above the approach roads, visible for miles. Franklin craned up at the grilles, tracing the power cables from the transformers up into the intricate mesh of metal coils that covered their surface. A line of red aircraft-warning beacons was already alight along the top strut, and Franklin assumed that the sign was part of the ground approach system of the city airport ten miles to the east.

Three minutes later, as he accelerated down the two-mile link of straight highway to the next clover-leaf, he saw the second of the giant signs looming up into the sky before him.

Changing down into the 40 m.p.h. lane, Franklin watched the great bulk of the second sign recede in his rear-view mirror. Although there were no graphic symbols among the wire coils covering the grilles, Hathaway's warnings still sounded in his ears. Without knowing why, he felt sure that the signs were not part of the airport approach system. Neither of them was in line with the principal air-lines. To justify the expense of siting them in the centre of the expressway—the second sign required elaborate angled buttresses to support it on the narrow island—obviously meant that their role related in some way to the traffic streams.

Two hundred yards away was a roadside auto-mart, and Franklin abruptly remembered that he needed some cigarettes. Swinging the car down the entrance ramp, he joined the queue passing the self-service dispenser at the far end of the rank. The auto-mart was packed with cars, each of the five purchasing ranks lined with tired-looking men hunched over their wheels.

Inserting his coins (paper money was no longer in circulation, unmanageable by the automats) he took a carton from the dispenser. This was the only brand of cigarettes available—in fact there was only one brand of everything—though giant economy packs were an alternative. Moving off, he opened the dashboard locker.

Inside, still sealed in their wrappers, were three other cartons.

A strong fish-like smell pervaded the house when he reached home, steaming out from the oven in the kitchen. Sniffing it uneagerly, Franklin took off his coat and hat. His wife was crouched over the TV set in the lounge. An announcer was dictating a stream of numbers, and Judith scribbled them down on a pad, occasionally cursing under her breath. 'What a muddle!' she snapped. 'He was talking so quickly I took only a few things down.'

'Probably deliberate,' Franklin commented. 'A new panel game?'

Judith kissed him on the cheek, discreetly hiding the ashtray loaded with cigarette butts and chocolate wrappings. 'Hello, darling, sorry not to have a drink ready for you. They've started this series of Spot Bargains, they give you a selection of things on which you get a ninety per cent trade-in discount at the local stores, if you're in the right area and have the right serial numbers. It's all terribly complicated.'

'Sounds good, though. What have you got?'

Judith peered at her checklist. 'Well, as far as I can see the only thing is the infra-red barbecue spit. But we have to be there before eight o'clock tonight. It's seven thirty already.'

'Then that's out. I'm tired, angel, I need something to eat.' When Judith started to protest he added firmly: 'Look, I don't want a new infra-red barbecue spit, we've only had this one for two months. Damn it, it's not even a different model.'

'But, darling, don't you see, it makes it cheaper if you

keep buying new ones. We'll have to trade ours in at the end of the year anyway, we signed the contract, and this way we save at least five pounds. These Spot Bargains aren't just a gimmick, you know. I've been glued to that set all day.' A note of irritation had crept into her voice, but Franklin stood his ground, doggedly ignoring the clock.

'Right, we lose five pounds. It's worth it.' Before she could remonstrate he said : 'Judith, please, you probably took the wrong number down anyway.' As she shrugged and went over to the bar he called : 'Make it a stiff one. I see we have health foods on the menu.'

'They're good for you, darling. You know you can't live on ordinary foods all the time. They don't contain any proteins or vitamins. You're always saying we ought to be like people in the old days and eat nothing but health foods.'

'I would, but they smell so awful.' Franklin lay back, nose in the glass of whisky, gazing at the darkened skyline outside.

A quarter of a mile away, gleaming out above the roof of the neighbourhood supermarket, were the five red beacon lights. Now and then, as the headlamps of the Spot Bargainers swung up across the face of the building, he could see the massive bulk of the sign clearly silhouetted against the evening sky.

'Judith!' He went into the kitchen and took her over to the window. 'That sign, just behind the supermarket. When did they put it up?'

'I don't know.' Judith peered at him. 'Why are you so worried, Robert? Isn't it something to do with the airport?'

Franklin stared at the dark hull of the sign. 'So everyone probably thinks.'

Carefully he poured his whisky into the sink.

After parking his car on the supermarket apron at seven o'clock the next morning, Franklin carefully emptied his pockets and stacked the coins in the dashboard locker. The supermarket was already busy with early morning shoppers and the line of thirty turnstiles clicked and slammed. Since the introduction of the '24-hour spending day' the shopping complex was never closed. The bulk of the shoppers were discount buyers, housewives contracted to make huge volume purchases of food, clothing and appliances against substantial overall price cuts, and forced to drive around all day from supermarket to supermarket, frantically trying to keep pace with their purchase schedules and grappling with the added incentives inserted to keep the schemes alive.

Many of the women had teamed up, and as Franklin walked over to the entrance a pack of them charged towards their cars, stuffing their pay slips into their bags and shouting at each other. A moment later their cars roared off in a convoy to the next marketing zone.

A large neon sign over the entrance listed the latest discount—a mere five per cent—calculated on the volume of turnover. The highest discounts, sometimes up to twenty-five per cent, were earned in the housing estates where junior white-collar workers lived. There, spending had a strong social incentive, and the desire to be the highest spender in the neighbourhood was given moral reinforcement by the system of listing all the names and their accumulating cash totals on a huge electric sign in the supermarket foyers. The higher the spender, the greater his contribution to the discounts enjoyed by others. The lowest spenders were regarded as social criminals, free-riding on the backs of others.

Luckily this system had yet to be adopted in Franklin's neighbourhood—not because the Professional men and their wives were able to exercise more discretion, but because their higher incomes allowed them to contract into more expensive discount schemes operated by the big department stores in the city.

Ten yards from the entrance Franklin paused, looking up at the huge metal sign mounted in an enclosure at the edge of the car park. Unlike the other signs and hoardings that proliferated everywhere, no attempt had been made to decorate it, or disguise the gaunt bare rectangle of riveted steel mesh. Power lines wound down its sides, and the concrete surface of the car park was crossed by a long scar where a cable had been sunk.

Franklin strolled along. Fifty feet from the sign he stopped and turned, realizing that he would be late for the hospital and needed a new carton of cigarettes. A dim but powerful humming emanated from the transformers below the sign, fading as he retraced his steps to the supermarket.

Going over to the automats in the foyer, he felt for his change, then whistled sharply when he rememberd why he had deliberately emptied his pockets.

'Hathaway!' he said, loudly enough for two shoppers to stare at him. Reluctant to look directly at the sign, he watched its reflection in one of the glass door-panes, so that any subliminal message would be reversed.

Almost certainly he had received two distinct signals —'Keep Away' and 'Buy Cigarettes'. The people who normally parked their cars along the perimeter of the apron were avoiding the area under the enclosure, the cars describing a loose semi-circle fifty feet around it.

He turned to the janitor sweeping out the foyer. 'What's that sign for?'

The man leaned on his broom, gazing dully at the sign. 'No idea,' he said. 'Must be something to do with the airport.' He had a fresh cigarette in his mouth, but his right hand reached to his hip pocket and pulled out a pack. He drummed the second cigarette absently on his thumb-nail as Franklin walked away.

Everyone entering the supermarket was buying cigarettes.

Cruising quietly along the 40 m.p.h. lane, Franklin began to take a closer interest in the landscape around him. Usually he was either too tired or too preoccupied to do more than think about his driving, but now he examined the expressway methodically, scanning the roadside cafés for any smaller versions of the new signs. A host of neon displays covered the doorways and windows, but most of them seemed innocuous, and he turned his attention to the larger billboards erected along the open stretches of the expressway. Many of these were as high as four-storey houses, elaborate three-dimensional devices in which giant housewives with electric eyes and teeth jerked and postured around their ideal kitchens, neon flashes exploding from their smiles.

The areas on either side of the expressway were wasteland, continuous junkyards filled with cars and trucks, washing machines and refrigerators, all perfectly workable but jettisoned by the economic pressure of the succeeding waves of discount models. Their intact chrome hardly tarnished, the metal shells and cabinets glittered in the sunlight. Nearer the city the billboards were sufficiently close together to hide them but now and then, as he slowed to approach one of the flyovers, Franklin caught a glimpse of the huge pyramids of metal, gleaming silently like the refuse grounds of some forgotten El Dorado.

That evening Hathaway was waiting for him as he came down the hospital steps. Franklin waved him across the court, then led the way quickly to his car.

'What's the matter, Doctor?' Hathaway asked as Franklin wound up the windows and glanced around the lines of parked cars. 'Is someone after you?'

Franklin laughed sombrely. 'I don't know. I hope not, but if what you say is right, I suppose there is.'

Hathaway leaned back with a chuckle, propping one knee up on the dashboard. 'So you've seen something, Doctor, after all.'

'Well, I'm not sure yet, but there's just a chance you may be right. This morning at the Fairlawne super-market . . .' He broke off, uneasily remembering the huge black sign and the abrupt way in which he had turned back to the supermarket as he approached it, then de-scribed his encounter.

Hathaway nodded. 'I've seen the sign there. It's big, but not as big as some that are going up. They're build-ing them everywhere now. All over the city. What are you going to do, Doctor?'

Franklin gripped the wheel tightly. Hathaway's thinly veiled amusement irritated him. 'Nothing, of course. Damn it, it may be just auto-suggestion, you've probably got me imagining——'

Hathaway sat up with a jerk. 'Don't be absurd, Doc-tor! If you can't believe your own senses what chance have you left? They're invading your brain, if you don't defend yourself they'll take it over completely! We've got to act now, before we're all paralysed.'

Wearily Franklin raised one hand to restrain him. 'Just a minute. Assuming that these signs *are* going up every-where, what would be their object? Apart from wasting the enormous amount of capital invested in all the other millions of signs and billboards, the amounts of discre-tionary spending power still available must be infinitesi-mal. Some of the present mortgage and discount schemes reach half a century ahead. A big trade war would be disastrous.'

'Quite right, Doctor,' Hathaway rejoined evenly, 'but you're forgetting one thing. What would supply that extra spending power? A big increase in production.

Already they've started to raise the working day from twelve hours to fourteen. In some of the appliance plants around the city Sunday working is being introduced as a norm. Can you visualize it, Doctor—a seven-day week, everyone with at least three jobs.'

Franklin shook his head. 'People won't stand for it.'

'They will. Within the last twenty-five years the gross national product has risen by fifty per cent, but so have the average hours worked. Ultimately we'll all be working and spending twenty-four hours a day, seven days a week. No one will dare refuse. Think what a slump would mean—millions of lay-offs, people with time on their hands and nothing to spend it on. Real leisure, not just time spent buying things,' He seized Franklin by the shoulder. 'Well, Doctor, are you going to join me?'

Franklin freed himself. Half a mile away, partly hidden by the four-storey bulk of the Pathology Department, was the upper half of one of the giant signs, workmen still crawling across its girders. The airlines over the city had deliberately been routed away from the hospital, and the sign obviously had no connection with approaching aircraft.

'Isn't there a prohibition on—what did they call it— subliminal living? How can the unions accept it?'

'The fear of a slump. You know the new economic dogmas. Unless output rises by a steady inflationary five per cent the economy is stagnating. Ten years ago increased efficiency alone would raise output, but the advantages there are minimal now and only one thing is left. More work. Subliminal advertising will provide the spur.'

'What are you planning to do?'

'I can't tell you, Doctor, unless you accept equal responsibility for it.'

'That sounds rather Quixotic,' Franklin commented. 'Tilting at windmills. You won't be able to chop those things down with an axe.'

'I won't try.' Hathaway opened the door. 'Don't wait too long to make up your mind, Doctor. By then it may not be yours to make up.' With a wave he was gone.

On the way home Franklin's scepticism returned. The idea of the conspiracy was preposterous, and the economic arguments were too plausible. As usual, though, there had been a hook in the soft bait Hathaway dangled before him—Sunday working. His own consultancy had been extended into Sunday morning with his appointment as visiting factory doctor to one of the automobile plants that had started Sunday shifts. But instead of resenting this incursion into his already meagre hours of leisure he had been glad. For one frightening reason—he needed the extra income.

Looking out over the lines of scurrying cars, he noticed that at least a dozen of the great signs had been erected along the expressway. As Hathaway had said, more were going up everywhere, rearing over the supermarkets in the housing developments like rusty metal sails.

Judith was in the kitchen when he reached home, watching the TV programme on the hand-set over the cooker. Franklin climbed past a big cardboard carton, its seals still unbroken, which blocked the doorway, kissed her on the cheek as she scribbled numbers down on her pad. The pleasant odour of pot-roast chicken—or, rather a gelatine dummy of a chicken fully flavoured and free of any toxic or nutritional properties—mollified his irritation at finding her still playing the Spot Bargains.

He tapped the carton with his foot. 'What's this?'

'No idea, darling, something's always coming these days, I can't keep up with it all.' She peered through the glass door at the chicken—an economy twelve-pounder, the size of a turkey, with stylized legs and wings and an enormous breast, most of which would be discarded at the end of the meal (there were no dogs or cats these days, the crumbs from the rich man's table saw to that) —and then glanced at him pointedly.

'You look rather worried, Robert. Bad day?'

Franklin murmured noncommittally. The hours spent trying to detect false clues in the faces of the Spot Bargain announcers had sharpened Judith's perceptions. He felt a pang of sympathy for the legion of husbands similarly outmatched.

'Have you been talking to that crazy beatnik again?'

'Hathaway? As a matter of fact I have. He's not all that crazy.' He stepped backwards into the carton, almost spilling his drink. 'Well, what is this thing? As I'll be working for the next fifty Sundays to pay for it I'd like to find out.'

He searched the sides, finally located the label. 'A TV set? Judith, do we need another one? We've already got three. Lounge, dining-room and the hand-set. What's the fourth for?'

'The guest-room, dear, don't get so excited. We can't leave a hand-set in the guest-room, it's rude. I'm trying to economize, but four TV sets is the bare minimum. All the magazines say so.'

'And three radios?' Franklin stared irritably at the carton. 'If we do invite a guest here now much time is he going to spend alone in his room watching television? Judith, we've got to call a halt. It's not as if these things were free, or even cheap. Anyway, television is a total waste of time. There's only one programme. It's ridiculous to have four sets.'

'Robert, there are four channels.'

'But only the commercials are different.' Before Judith could reply the telephone rang. Franklin lifted the kitchen receiver, listened to the gabble of noise that poured from it. At first he wondered whether this was some off-beat prestige commercial, then realized it was Hathaway in a manic swing.

'Hathaway!' he shouted back. 'Relax, for God's sake! What's the matter now?'

'—Doctor, you'll have to believe me this time. I climbed on to one of the islands with a stroboscope, they've got hundreds of high-speed shutters blasting away like machine-guns straight into people's faces and they can't see a thing, it's fantastic! The next big campaign's going to be cars and TV sets, they're trying to swing a two-month model change—can you imagine it, Doctor, a new car every two months? God Almighty, it's just——'

Franklin waited impatiently as the five-second commercial break cut in (all telephone calls were free, the length of the commercial extending with range—for long-distance calls the ratio of commercial to conversation was as high as 10:1, the participants desperately trying to get a word in edgeways between the interminable interruptions), but just before it ended he abruptly put the telephone down, then removed the receiver from the cradle.

Judith came over and took his arm. 'Robert, what's the matter? You look terribly strained.'

Franklin picked up his drink and walked through into the lounge. 'It's just Hathaway. As you say, I'm getting a little too involved with him. He's starting to prey on my mind.'

He looked at the dark outline of the sign over the supermarket, its red warning lights glowing in the night sky. Blank and nameless, like an area for ever closed-off in an insane mind, what frightened him was its total anonymity.

'Yet I'm not sure,' he muttered. 'So much of what Hathaway says makes sense. These subliminal techniques are the sort of last-ditch attempt you'd expect from an over-capitalized industrial system.'

He waited for Judith to reply, then looked up at her. She stood in the centre of the carpet, hands folded limply, her sharp, intelligent face curiously dull and blunted. He followed her gaze out over the rooftops, then with an effort turned his head and quickly switched on the TV set.

'Come on,' he said grimly. 'Let's watch television. God, we're going to need that fourth set.'

A week later Franklin began to compile his inventory. He saw nothing more of Hathaway; as he left the hospital in the evening the familiar scruffy figure was absent. When the first of the explosions sounded dimly around the city and he read of the attempts to sabotage the giant signs he automatically assumed that Hathaway was responsible, but later he heard on a newscast that the detonations had been set off by construction workers excavating foundations.

More of the signs appeared over the rooftops, isolated on the palisaded islands near the suburban shopping centres. Already there were over thirty on the ten mile route from the hospital, standing shoulder to shoulder over the speeding cars like giant dominoes. Franklin had given up his attempt to avoid looking at them, but the slim possibility that the explosions might be Hathaway's counter-attack kept his suspicions alive.

He began his inventory after hearing the newscast, and discovered that in the previous fortnight he and Judith had traded in their

Car (previous model 2 months old)

2 TV sets (4 months)

Power mower (7 months)

Electric cooker (5 months)

Hair dryer (4 months)

Refrigerator (3 months)

2 radios (7 months)
Record player (5 months)
Cocktail bar (8 months)

Half these purchases had been made by himself, but
exactly when he could never recall realizing at the time.
The car, for example, he had left in the garage near the
hospital to be greased, that evening had signed for the
new model as he sat at its wheel, accepting the saleman's
assurance that the depreciation on the two-month trade-
in was virtually less than the cost of the grease-job. Ten
minutes later, as he sped along the expressway, he suddenly realized that he had bought a new car. Similarly,
the TV sets had been replaced by identical models after
developing the same irritating interference pattern (curiously, the new sets also displayed the pattern, but as the
salesman assured them, this promptly vanished two days
later.) Not once had he actually decided of his own
volition that he wanted something and then gone out to
a store and bought it!

He carried the inventory around with him, adding to
it as necessary, quietly and without protest analysing
these new sales techniques, wondering whether total
capitulation might be the only way of defeating them.
As long as he kept up even a token resistance, the inflationary growth curve would show a controlled annual
ten per cent climb. With that resistance removed, however, it would begin to rocket upwards out of control . . .

Driving home from the hospital two months later, he
saw one of the signs for the first time.

He was in the 40 m.p.h. lane, unable to keep up with
the flood of new cars, and had just passed the second of
the three clover-leaves when the traffic half a mile away
began to slow down. Hundreds of cars had driven up on
to the grass verge, and a crowd was gathering around
one of the signs. Two small black figures were climbing

up the metal face, and a series of grid-like patterns of light flashed on and off, illuminating the evening air. The patterns were random and broken, as if the sign was being tested for the first time.

Relieved that Hathaway's suspicions had been completely groundless, Franklin turned off on to the soft shoulder, then walked forward through the spectators as the lights stuttered in their faces. Below, behind the steel palisades around the island, was a large group of police and engineers, craning up at the men scaling the sign a hundred feet over their heads.

Suddenly Franklin stopped, the sense of relief fading instantly. Several of the police on the ground were armed with shotguns, and the two policemen climbing the sign carried submachine-guns slung over their shoulders. They were converging on a third figure, crouched by a switch-box on the penultimate tier, a bearded man in a grimy shirt, a bare knee poking through his jeans.

Hathaway!

Franklin hurried towards the island, the sign hissing and spluttering, fuses blowing by the dozen.

Then the flicker of lights cleared and steadied, blazing out continuously, and together the crowd looked up at the decks of brilliant letters. The phrases, and every combination of them possible, were entirely familiar, and Franklin knew that he had been reading them for weeks as he passed up and down the expressway.

BUY NOW BUY NOW BUY NOW BUY NOW BUY
NEW CAR NOW NEW CAR NOW NEW CAR NOW
YES YES YES YES YES YES YES YES YES YES

Sirens blaring, two patrol cars swung on to the verge through the crowd and plunged across the damp grass. Police spilled from their doors, batons in their hands, and quickly began to force back the crowd. Franklin held his ground as they approached, stared to say: 'Officer, I know the man——' but the policeman punched him in the chest with the flat of his hand. Winded, he stumbled back among the cars, and leaned helplessly against a fender as the police began to break the windshields, the hapless drivers protesting angrily, those farther back rushing for their vehicles.

The noise fell away when one of the submachine-guns fired a brief roaring burst, then rose in a massive gasp as Hathaway, arms outstretched, let out a cry of triumph and pain, and jumped.

'But, Robert, what does it really matter?' Judith asked as Franklin sat inertly in the lounge the next morning. 'I know it's tragic for his wife and daughter, but Hathaway was in the grip of an obsession. If he hated advertising signs so much why didn't he dynamite those we *can* see, instead of worrying so much about those we can't?'

Franklin stared at the TV screen, hoping the programme would distract him.

'Hathaway was *right*,' he said.

'Was he? Advertising is here to stay. We've no real freedom of choice, anyway. We can't spend more than we can afford, the finance companies soon clamp down.'

'Do you accept that?' Franklin went over to the window. A quarter of a mile away, in the centre of the estate, another of the signs was being erected. It was due east from them, and in the early morning light the shadows of its rectangular superstructure fell across the garden, reaching almost to the steps of the french windows at his feet. As a concession to the neighbourhood, and perhaps to allay any suspicions while it was being erected by an appeal to petty snobbery, the lower sections had been encased in mock-Tudor panelling.

Franklin stared at it, counting the half-dozen police lounging by their patrol cars as the construction gang unloaded the prefabricated grilles from a truck. He looked at the sign by the supermarket, trying to repress his memories of Hathaway and the pathetic attempts the man had made to convince Franklin and gain his help.

He was still standing there an hour later when Judith came in, putting on her hat and coat, ready to visit the supermarket.

Franklin followed her to the door. 'I'll drive you down there, Judith. I have to see about booking a new car. The next models are coming out at the end of the month. With luck we'll get one of the early deliveries.'

They walked out into the trim drive, the shadows of the signs swinging across the quiet neighbourhood as the day progressed, sweeping over the heads of the people on their way to the supermarket like the blades of enormous scythes.

Again at night Mason heard the sounds of the approaching sea, the muffled thunder of breakers rolling up the near-by streets. Roused from his sleep, he ran out into the moonlight, where the white-framed houses stood like sepulchres among the washed concrete courts. Two hundred yards away the waves plunged and boiled, sluicing in and out across the pavement. Foam seethed through the picket fences, and the broken spray filled the air with the wine-sharp tang of brine.

Off-shore the deeper swells of the open sea rode across the roofs of the submerged houses, the white-caps cleft by isolated chimneys. Leaping back as the cold foam stung his feet, Mason glanced at the house where his wife lay sleeping. Each night the sea moved a few yards nearer, a hissing guillotine across the empty lawns.

For half an hour Mason watched the waves vault among the rooftops. The luminous surf cast a pale nimbus on the clouds racing overhead on the dark wind, and covered his hands with a waxy sheen.

At last the waves began to recede, and the deep bowl of illuminated water withdrew down the emptying streets, disgorging the lines of houses in the moonlight. Mason ran forwards across the expiring bubbles, but the sea shrank away from him, disappearing around the corners of the houses, sliding below the garage doors. He sprinted to the end of the road as a last glow was carried across the sky beyond the spire of the church. Exhausted, Mason returned to his bed, the sound of the dying waves filling his head as he slept.

'I saw the sea again last night,' he told his wife at breakfast.

Quietly, Miriam said: 'Richard, the nearest sea is a thousand miles away.' She watched her husband for a moment, her pale fingers straying to the coil of black hair lying against her neck. 'Go out into the drive and look. There's no sea.'

'Darling, I *saw* it.'

'Richard———!'

Mason stood up, and with slow deliberation raised his palms. 'Miriam, I felt the spray on my hands. The waves were breaking around my feet. I wasn't dreaming.'

'You must have been.' Miriam leaned against the door, as if trying to exclude the strange nightworld of her husband. With her long raven hair framing her oval face, and the scarlet dressing-gown open to reveal her slender neck and white breast, she reminded Mason of a Pre-Raphaelite heroine in an Arthurian pose. 'Richard, you must see Dr Clifton. It's beginning to frighten me.'

Mason smiled, his eyes searching the distant rooftops above the trees. 'I shouldn't worry. What's happening is really very simple. At night I hear the sounds of the sea, I go out and watch the waves in the moonlight, and then come back to bed.' He paused, a flush of fatigue on his face. Tall and slimly built, Mason was still convalescing from the illness which had kept him at home for the previous six months. 'It's curious, though,' he resumed, 'the water is remarkably luminous. I should guess its salinity is well above normal———'

'But Richard . . .' Miriam looked around helplessly, her husband's calmness exhausting her. 'The sea isn't *there*; it's only in your mind. No one else can see it.'

Mason nodded, hands lost in his pockets. 'Perhaps no one else has heard it yet.'

Leaving the breakfast-room, he went into his study. The couch on which he had slept during his illness still stood against the corner, his bookcase beside it. Mason sat down, taking a large fossil mollusc from a shelf. During the winter, when he had been confined to bed, the smooth trumpet-shaped conch, with its endless associations of ancient seas and drowned strands, had provided him with unlimited pleasure, a bottomless cornucopia of image and reverie. Cradling it reassuringly in his hands, as exquisite and ambiguous as a fragment of Greek sculpture found in a dry riverbed, he reflected that it seemed like a capsule of time, the condensation of another universe. He could almost believe that the midnight sea which haunted his sleep had been released from the shell when he had inadvertently scratched one of its helixes.

Miriam followed him into the room and briskly drew the curtains, as if aware that Mason was returning to the twilight world of his sick-bed. She took his shoulders in her hands.

'Richard, listen. Tonight, when you hear the waves, wake me and we'll go out together.'

Gently, Mason disengaged himself. 'Whether you see it or not is irrelevant, Miriam. The fact is that I see it.'

Later, walking down the street, Mason reached the point where he had stood the previous night, watching the waves break and roll towards him. The sounds of placid domestic activity came from the houses he had seen submerged. The grass on the lawns was bleached by the July heat, and sprays rotated in the bright sunlight, casting rainbows in the vivid air. Undisturbed since the rainstorms in the early spring, the long summer's dust lay between the wooden fences and water hydrants.

The street, one of a dozen suburban boulevards on the perimeter of the town, ran north-west for some three hundred yards and then joined the open square of the neighbourhood shopping centre. Mason shielded his eyes and looked out at the clock tower of the library and the church spire, identifying the protuberances which had risen from the steep swells of the open sea. All were in exactly the positions he remembered.

The road shelved slightly as it approached the shopping centre, and by a curious coincidence marked the margins of the beach which would have existed if the area had been flooded. A mile or so from the town, this shallow ridge, which formed part of the rim of a large natural basin enclosing the alluvial plain below, culminated in a small chalk outcropping. Although it was partly hidden by the intervening houses, Mason now recognized it clearly as the promontory which had reared like a citadel above the sea. The deep swells had rolled against its flanks, sending up immense plumes of spray that fell back with almost hypnotic slowness upon the receding water. At night the promontory seemed larger and more gaunt, as uneroded bastion against the sea. One evening, Mason promised himself, he would go out to the promontory and let the waves wake him as he slept on the peak.

A car moved past, the driver watching Mason curiously as he stood in the middle of the road, head raised to the air. Not wishing to appear any more eccentric than he was already considered—the solitary, abstracted husband of the beautiful but childless Mrs Mason—Mason turned into the avenue which ran along the ridge. As he approached the distant outcropping he glanced over the hedges for any signs of water-logged gardens or stranded cars. The houses had been inundated by the floodwater.

The first visions of the sea had come to Mason only three weeks earlier, but he was already convinced of their absolute validity. He recognized that after its nightly withdrawal the water failed to leave any mark on the hundreds of houses it submerged, and he felt no alarm for the drowned people who were, presumably, as he watched the luminous waves break across the rooftops, sleeping undisturbed in the sea's immense liquid locker. Despite this paradox, it was his complete conviction of the sea's reality that had made him admit to Miriam that he had woken one night to the sound of waves outside the window and gone out to find the sea rolling across the neighbourhood streets and houses. At first she had merely smiled at him, accepting this illustration of his strange private world. Then, three nights later, she had woken to the sound of him latching the door on his return, bewildered by his pumping chest and perspiring face.

From then on she spent all day looking over her shoulder through the window for any signs of the sea. What worried her as much as the vision itself was Mason's complete calm in the face of this terrifying unconscious apocalypse.

Tired by his walk, Mason sat down on a low ornamental wall, screened from the surrounding houses by the rhododendron bushes. For a few minutes he played with the dust at his feet, stirring the white grains with a branch. Although formless and passive, the dust shared something of the same evocative qualities of the fossil mollusc, radiating a curious compacted light.

In front of him, the road curved and dipped, the incline carrying it away on to the fields below. The chalk shoulder, covered by a mantle of green turf, rose into the clear sky. A metal shack had been erected on the slope, and a small group of figures moved about the entrance of a mine-shaft, adjusting a wooden hoist. Wishing that he had brought his wife's car, Mason watched the diminutive figures disappear one by one into the shaft.

The image of this elusive pantomime remained with him all day in the library, overlaying his memories of the dark waves rolling across the midnight streets. What sustained Mason was his conviction that others would soon also become aware of the sea.

When he went to bed that night he found Miriam sitting fully dressed in the armchair by the window, her face composed into an expression of calm determination.

'What are you doing?' he asked.

'Waiting.'

'For what?'

'The sea. Don't worry, simply ignore me and go to sleep. I don't mind sitting here with the light out.'

'Miriam . . .' Wearily, Mason took one of her slender hands and tried to draw her from the chair. 'Darling, what on earth will this achieve?'

'Isn't it obvious?'

Mason sat down on the foot of the bed. For some reason, not wholly concerned with the wish to protect her, he wanted to keep his wife from the sea. 'Miriam, don't you understand? I might not actually *see* it, in the literal sense. It might be . . .' he extemporized . . . 'an hallucination, or a dream.'

Miriam shook her head, hands clasped on the arms of the chair. 'I don't think it is. Anyway, I want to find out.'

Mason lay back on the bed. 'I wonder whether you're approaching this the right way——'

Miriam sat forward. 'Richard, you're taking it all so calmly; you accept this vision as if it were a strange headache. That's what frightens me. If you were really terrified by this sea I wouldn't worry, but . . .'

Half an hour later he fell asleep in the darkened room, Miriam's slim face watching him from the shadows.

Waves murmured, outside the windows the distant swish of racing foam drew him from sleep, the muffled thunder of rollers and the sounds of deep water drummed at his ears. Mason climbed out of bed, and dressed quickly as the hiss of receding water sounded up the street. In the corner, under the light reflected from the distant foam, Miriam lay asleep in the armchair, a bar of moonlight across her throat.

His bare feet soundless on the pavement, Mason ran towards the waves. He stumbled across the glistening tideline as one of the breakers struck with a guttural roar. On his knees, Mason felt the cold brilliant water, seething with animalcula, spurt across his chest and shoulders, slacken and then withdraw, sucked like a gleaming floor into the mouth of the next breaker. His wet suit clinging to him like a drowned animal, Mason stared out across the sea. In the moonlight the white houses advanced into the water like the palazzos of a spectral Venice, mausoleums on the causeways of some island necropolis. Only the church spire was still visible. The water rode in to its high tide, a further twenty yards down the street, the spray carried almost to the Mason's house.

Mason waited for an interval between two waves and then waded through the shallows to the avenue which wound towards the distant headland. By now the water had crossed the roadway, swilling over the dark lawns and slapping at the doorsteps.

Half a mile from the headland he heard the great surge and sigh of the deeper water. Out of breath, he leaned against a fence as the cold foam cut across his legs, pulling him with its undertow. Illuminated by the racing clouds, he saw the pale figure of a woman standing above the sea on a stone parapet at the cliff's edge, her black robe lifting behind her in the wind, her long hair white in the moonlight. Far below her feet, the luminous waves leapt and vaulted like acrobats.

Mason ran along the pavement, losing sight of her as the road curved and the houses intervened. The water slackened and he caught a last glimpse of the woman's icy-white profile through the spray. Turning, the tide began to ebb and fade, and the sea shrank away between the houses, draining the night of its light and motion.

As the last bubbles dissolved on the damp pavement, Mason searched the headland, but the luminous figure had gone. His damp clothes dried themselves as he walked back through the empty streets. A last tang of brine was carried away off the hedges on the midnight air.

The next morning he told Miriam : 'It *was* a dream, after all. I think the sea has gone now. Anyway, I saw nothing last night.'

'Thank heavens, Richard. Are you sure?'

'I'm certain.' Mason smiled encouragingly. 'Thanks for keeping watch over me.'

'I'll sit up tonight as well.' She held up her hand. 'I insist. I feel all right after last night, and I want to drive this thing away, once and for all.' She frowned over the coffee cups. 'It's strange, but once or twice I think I heard the sea too. It sounded very old and blind, like something waking again after millions of years.'

On his way to the library, Mason made a detour towards the chalk outcropping, and parked the car where he had seen the moonlit figure of the white-haired woman watching the sea. The sunlight fell on the pale turf, illuminating the mouth of the mine-shaft, around which the same desultory activity was taking place.

For the next fifteen minutes Mason drove in and out of the tree-lined avenues, peering over the hedges at the kitchen windows. Almost certainly she would live in one of the nearby houses, still wearing her black robe beneath a housecoat.

Later, at the library, he recognized a car he had seen on the headland. The driver, an elderly tweed-suited man, was examining the display cases of local geological finds.

'Who was that?' he asked Fellowes, the keeper of antiquities, as the car drove off. 'I've seen him on the cliffs.'

'Professor Goodhart, one of the party of paleontologists. Apparently they've uncovered an interesting bone-bed.' Fellowes gestured at the collection of femurs and jaw-bone fragments. 'With luck we may get a few pieces from them.'

Mason stared at the bones, aware of a sudden closing of the parallax within his mind.

Each night, as the sea emerged from the dark streets and the waves rolled farther towards the Masons' home, he would wake beside his sleeping wife and go out into the surging air, wading through the deep water towards the headland. There he would see the white-haired woman on the cliff's edge, her face raised above the roaring spray. Always he failed to reach her before the tide turned, and would kneel exhausted on the wet pavements as the drowned streets rose around him.

Once a police patrol car found him in its headlights, slumped against a gate-post in an open drive. On another night he forgot to close the front door when he returned. All through breakfast Miriam watched him with her old wariness, noticing the shadows which encircled his eyes like manacles.

'Richard, I think you should stop going to the library. You look worn out. It isn't that sea dream again?'

Mason shook his head, forcing a tired smile. 'No, that's finished with. Perhaps I've been over-working.'

Miriam held his hands. 'Did you fall over yesterday?' She examined Mason's palms. 'Darling, they're still *raw*! You must have grazed them only a few hours ago. Can't you remember?'

Abstracted, Mason invented some tale to satisfy her, then carried his coffee into the study and stared at the morning haze which lay across the rooftops, a soft lake of opacity that followed the same contours as the midnight sea. The mist dissolved in the sunlight, and for a moment the diminishing reality of the normal world reasserted itself, filling him with a poignant nostalgia.

Without thinking, he reached out to the fossil conch on the bookshelf, but involuntarily his hand withdrew before touching it.

Miriam stood beside him. 'Hateful thing,' she commented. 'Tell me, Richard, what do you think caused your dream?'

Mason shrugged. 'Perhaps it was a sort of memory . . .' He wondered whether to tell Miriam of the waves which he still heard in his sleep, and of the white-haired woman on the cliff's edge who seemed to beckon to him. But like all women Miriam believed that there was room for only one enigma in her husband's life. By an inversion of logic he felt that his dependence on his wife's private income, and the loss of self-respect, gave him the right to withhold something of himself from her.

'Richard, what's the matter?'

In his mind the spray opened like a diaphanous fan and the enchantress of the waves turned towards him.

Waist-high, the sea pounded across the lawn in a whirlpool. Mason pulled off his jacket and flung it into the water, and then waded out into the street. Higher than ever before, the waves had at last reached his house, breaking over the doorstep, but Mason had forgotten his wife. His attention was fixed upon the headland, which was lashed by a continuous storm of spray, almost obscuring the figure standing on its crest.

As Mason pressed on, sometimes sinking to his shoulders, shoals of luminous algae swarmed in the water around him. His eyes smarted in the saline air. He reached the lower slopes of the headland almost exhausted, and fell to his knees.

High above, he could hear the spray singing as it cut through the coigns of the cliff's edge, the deep base of the breakers overlayed by the treble of the keening air. Carried by the music, Mason climbed the flank of the headland, a thousand reflections of the moon in the breaking sea. As he reached the crest, the black robe hid the woman's face, but he could see her tall erect carriage and slender hips. Suddenly, without any apparent motion of her limbs, she moved away along the parapet.

'Wait!'

His shout was lost on the air. Mason ran forwards, and the figure turned and stared back at him. Her white hair swirled around her face like a spume of silver steam and then parted to reveal a face with empty eyes and notched mouth. A hand like a bundle of white sticks clawed towards him, and the figure rose through the whirling darkness like a gigantic bird.

Unaware whether the scream came from his own mouth or from this spectre, Mason stumbled back. Before he could catch himself he tripped over the wooden railing, and in a cackle of chains and pulleys fell backwards into the shaft, the sounds of the sea booming in its hurtling darkness.

After listening to the policeman's description, Professor Goodhart shook his head.

'I'm afraid not, sergeant. We've been working on the bed all week. No one's fallen down the shaft.' One of the flimsy wooden rails was swinging loosely in the crisp air. 'But thank you for warning me. I suppose we must build a heavier railing, if this fellow is wandering around in his sleep.'

'I don't think he'll bother to come up here,' the sergeant said. 'It's quite a climb.' As an afterthought he added: 'Down at the library where he works they said you'd found a couple of skeletons in the shaft yesterday. I know it's only two days since he disappeared, but one of them couldn't possibly be his?' The sergeant shrugged. 'If there was some natural acid, say . . .'

Professor Goodhart drove his heel into the chalky turf. 'Pure calcium carbonate, about a mile thick, laid down during the Triassic Period 200 million years ago when there was a large inland sea here. The skeletons we found yesterday, a man's and a woman's, belong to two Cro-Magnon fisher people who lived on the shore just before it dried up. I wish I could oblige you—it's quite a problem to understand how these Cro-Magnon relics found their way into the bone-bed. This shaft wasn't sunk until about thirty years ago. Still, that's my problem, not yours.'

Returning to the police car, the sergeant shook his head. As they drove off he looked out at the endless stretch of placid suburban homes.

'Apparently there was an ancient sea here once. A million years ago.' He picked a crumpled flannel jacket off the back seat. 'That reminds me, I know what Mason's coat smells of—brine.'

'Where, my God, *where* is he?'

Uttered in a tone of uncontrollable frustration as he paced up and down in front of the high-gabled window behind his desk, this *cri de coeur* of Dr Mellinger, Director of Green Hill Asylum, expressed the consternation of his entire staff at the mysterious disappearance of one of their patients. In the twelve hours which had elapsed since the escape, Dr Mellinger and his subordinates had progressed from surprise and annoyance to acute exasperation, and eventually to a mood of almost euphoric disbelief. To add insult to injury, not only had the patient, James Hinton, succeeded in becoming the first ever to escape from the asylum, but he had managed to do so without leaving any clues as to his route. Thus Dr Mellinger and his staff were tantalized by the possibility that Hinton had never escaped at all and was still safely within the confines of the asylum. At all events, everyone agreed that if Hinton *had* escaped, he had literally vanished into thin air.

However, one small consolation, Dr Mellinger reminded himself as he drummed his fingers on his desk, was that Hinton's disappearance had exposed the shortcomings of the asylum's security systems, and administered a salutary jolt to his heads of departments. As this hapless group, led by the Deputy Director, Dr Normand, filed into his office for the first of the morning's emergency conferences, Dr Mellinger cast a baleful glare at each in turn, but their sleepless faces remained mutely lowered to the carpeting, as if, despairing of finding Hinton anywhere else, they now sought his hiding-place in its deep ruby pile.

At least, Dr Mellinger reflected, only one patient had disappeared, a negative sentiment which assumed greater meaning in view of the outcry which would be raised from the world outside when it was discovered that a patient—obviously a homicidal lunatic—had remained at large for over twelve hours before the police were notified.

This decision not to inform the civil authorities, an error of judgement whose culpability seemed to mount as the hours passed, alone prevented Dr Mellinger from finding an immediate scapegoat—a convenient one would have been little Dr Mendelsohn of the Pathology Department, an unimportant branch of the asylum—and sacrificing him on the altar of his own indiscretion. His natural caution, and reluctance to yield an inch of ground unless compelled, had prevented Dr Mellinger from raising the general alarm during the first hours after Hinton's disappearance, when some doubt still remained whether the latter had actually left the asylum. Although the failure to find Hinton might have been interpreted as a reasonable indication that he had successfully escaped, Dr Mellinger had characteristically refused to accept such faulty logic.

By now, over twelve hours later, his miscaculation had become apparent. As the thin smirk on Dr Normand's face revealed, and as his other subordinates would soon realize, his directorship of the asylum was now at stake. Unless they found Hinton within a few hours he would be placed in an untenable position before both the civil authorities and the trustees.

However, Dr Mellinger reminded himself, it was not without the exercise of considerable guile and resource that he had become Director of Green Hill in the first place.

'Where *is* he?'

Shifting his emphasis from the first of these interrogatories to the second, as if to illustrate that the fruitless search for Hinton's whereabouts had been superseded by an examination of his total existential role in the unhappy farce of which he was the author and principal star, Dr Mellinger turned upon his three breakfastless subordinates.

'Well, have you found him? Don't sit there dozing, gentlemen! You may have had a sleepless night, but I have still to wake from the nightmare.' With this humourless shaft, Dr Mellinger flashed a mordant eye into the rhododendron-lined drive, as if hoping to catch a sudden glimpse of the vanished patient. 'Dr Redpath, your report, please.'

'The search is still continuing, Director.' Dr Redpath, the registrar of the asylum, was nominally in charge of security. 'We have examined the entire grounds, dormitory blocks, garages and outbuildings—even the patients are taking part—but every trace of Hinton has vanished. Reluctantly, I am afraid there is no alternative but to inform the police.'

'Nonsense.' Dr Mellinger took his seat behind the desk, arms outspread and eyes roving the bare top for a minuscule replica of the vanished patient. 'Don't be disheartened by your inability to discover him, Doctor. Until the search is complete we would be wasting the police's time to ask for their help.'

'Of course, Director,' Dr Normand rejoined smoothly, 'but on the other hand, as we have now proved that the missing patient is not within the boundaries of Green Hill, we can conclude, ergo, that he is outside them. In such an event is it perhaps rather a case of us helping the police?'

'Not at all, my dear Normand,' Dr Mellinger replied pleasantly. As he mentally elaborated his answer, he realized that he had never trusted or liked his deputy; given the first opportunity he would replace him, most conveniently with Redpath, whose blunders in the 'Hinton affair', as it could be designated, would place him for ever squarely below the Director's thumb. 'If there were any evidence of the means by which Hinton made his escape—knotted sheets or footprints in the flower-beds— we could assume that he was no longer within these walls. But no such evidence has been found. For all we know—in fact, everything points inescapably to this conclusion—the patient is still within the confines of Green Hill, indeed by rights still within his cell. The bars on the window were not cut, and the only way out was through the door, the keys to which remained in the passession of Dr Booth'—he indicated the third member of the trio, a slim young man with a worried expression—'throughout the period between the last contact with Hinton and the discovery of his disappearance. Dr Booth, as the physician actually responsible for Hinton, you are quite certain you were the last person to visit him?'

Dr Booth nodded reluctantly. His celebrity at having discovered Hinton's escape had long since turned sour. 'At seven o'clock, sir, during my evening round. But the last person to *see* Hinton was the duty nurse half an hour later. However, as no treatment had been prescribed— the patient had been admitted for observation—the door was not unlocked. Shortly after nine o'clock I decided to visit the patient——'

'Why?' Dr Mellinger placed the tips of his fingers together and constructed a cathedral spire and nave. 'This is one of the strangest aspects of the case, Doctor. Why should you have chosen, almost an hour and a half later, to leave your comfortable office on the ground floor and climb three flights of stairs merely to carry out a cursory inspection which could best be left to the duty staff? Your motives puzzle me, Doctor.'

'But, Director——!' Dr Booth was almost on his feet. 'Surely you don't suspect me of colluding in Hinton's escape? I assure you——'

'Doctor, please.' Dr Mellinger raised a smooth white hand. 'Nothing could be further from my mind. Perhaps I should have said: your *unconscious* motives.'

Again the unfortunate Booth protested: 'Director, there were no unconscious motives. I admit I can't remember precisely what prompted me to see Hinton, but it was some perfectly trivial reason. I hardly knew the patient.'

Dr Mellinger bent forwards across the desk. 'That is exactly what I meant, Doctor. To be precise, you did not know Hinton at all.' Dr Mellinger gazed at the distorted reflection of himself in the silver ink-stand. 'Tell me, Dr Booth, how would you describe Hinton's appearance?'

Booth hesitated. 'Well, he was of . . . medium height, if I remember, with . . . yes, brown hair and a pale complexion. His eyes were—I should have to refresh my memory from the file, Director.'

Dr Mellinger nodded. He turned to Redpath. 'Could you describe him, Doctor?'

'I'm afraid not, sir. I never saw the patient.' He gestured to the Deputy Director. 'I believe Dr Normand interviewed him on admission.'

With an effort Dr Normand cast into his memory. 'It was probably my assistant. If I remember, he was a man of average build with no distinguishing features. Neither short, nor tall. Stocky, one might say.' He pursed his lips. 'Yes. Or rather, no. I'm certain it was my assistant.'

'How interesting.' Dr Mellinger had visibly revived, the gleams of ironic humour which flashed from his eyes revealed some potent inner transformation. The burden of irritations and frustrations which had plagued him for the past day seemed to have been lifted. 'Does this mean, Dr Normand, that this entire institution has been mobilized in a search for a man whom no one here could recognize even if they found him? You surprise me, my dear Normand. I was under the impression that you were a man of cool and analytical intelligence, but in your search for Hinton you are obviously employing more arcane powers.'

'But, Director! I cannot be expected to memorize the face of every patient——'

'Enough, enough!' Dr Mellinger stood up with a flourish, and resumed his circuit of the carpet. 'This is all very disturbing. Obviously the whole relationship between Green Hill and its patients must be re-examined. Our patients are not faceless ciphers, gentlemen, but the possessors of unique and vital identities. If we regard them as nonentities and fail to invest them with any personal characteristics, is it surprising that they should seem to disappear? I suggest that we put aside the next few days and dedicate them to a careful re-appraisal. Let us scrutinize all those facile assumptions we make so readily.' Impelled by this vision, Dr Mellinger stepped into the light pouring through the window, as if to expose himself to this new revelation. 'Yes, this is the task which lies before us now; from its successful conclusion will emerge a new Green Hill, a Green Hill without shadows and conspiracies, where patients and physicians stand before each other in mutual trust and responsibility.'

A pregnant silence fell at the conclusion of this homily. At last Dr Redpath cleared his throat, reluctant to disturb Dr Mellinger's sublime communion with himself. 'And Hinton, sir?'

'Hinton? Ah, yes.' Dr Mellinger turned to face them, like a bishop about to bless his congregation. 'Let us see Hinton as an illustration of this process of self-examination, a focus of our re-appraisal.'

'So the search should continue, sir?' Redpath pressed.

'Of course.' For a moment Dr Mellinger's attention wandered. 'Yes, we must find Hinton. He is here some-

where; his essence pervades Green Hill, a vast metaphysical conundrum. Solve it, gentlemen, and you will
have solved the mystery of his disappearance.'

For the next hour Dr Mellinger paced the carpet alone,
now and then warming his hands at the low fire below
the mantelpiece. Its few flames entwined in the chimney
like the ideas playing around the periphery of his mind.
At last, he felt, a means of breaking through the impasse
had offered itself. He had always been certain that Hinton's miraculous disappearance represented more than a
simple problem of breached security, and was a symbol
of something grievously at fault with the very foundations of Green Hill.

Pursuing these thoughts, Dr Mellinger left his office and
made his way down to the floor below which housed the
administrative department. The offices were deserted; the
entire staff of the building was taking part in the search.
Occasionally the querulous cries of the patients demand-
ing their breakfasts drifted across the warm, insulated
air. Fortunately the walls were thick, and the rates
charged by the asylum high enough to obviate the need
for over-crowding.

Green Hill Asylum (motto, and principal attraction:
'There is a Green Hill Far, Far Away') was one of those
institutions which are patronized by the wealthier members of the community and in effect serve the role of
private prisons. In such places are confined all those mis-
creant or unfortunate relatives whose presence would
otherwise be a burden or embarrassment: the impor-
tunate widows of blacksheep sons, senile maiden aunts,
elderly bachelor cousins paying the price for their
romantic indiscretions—in short, all those abandoned
casualties of the army of privilege. As far as the patrons
of Green Hill were concerned, maximum security came
first, treatment, if given at all, a bad second. Dr Mel-

linger's patients had disappeared conveniently from the world, and as long as they remained in this distant limbo those who paid the bills were satisfied. All this made Hinton's escape particularly dangerous.

Stepping through the open doorway of Normand's office, Dr Mellinger ran his eye cursorily around the room. On the desk, hastily opened, was a slim file containing a few documents and a photograph.

For a brief moment Dr Mellinger gazed abstractedly at the file. Then, after a discreet glance into the corridor, he slipped it under his arm and retraced his steps up the empty staircase.

Outside, muted by the dark groves of rhododendrons, the sounds of search and pursuit echoed across the grounds. Opening the file on his desk, Dr Mellinger stared at the photograph, which happened to be lying upside down. Without straightening it, he studied the amorphous features. The nose was straight, the forehead and cheeks symmetrical, the ears a little oversize, but in its inverted position the face lacked any cohesive identity.

Suddenly, as he started to read the file, Dr Mellinger was filled with a deep sense of resentment. The entire subject of Hinton and the man's precarious claims to reality overwhelmed him with a profound nausea. He refused to accept that this mindless cripple with his anonymous features could have been responsible for the confusion and anxiety of the previous day. Was it possible that these few pieces of paper constituted this meagre individual's full claim to reality?

Flinching slightly from the touch of the file to his fingers, Dr Mellinger carried it across to the fire-place. Averting his face, he listened with a deepening sense of relief as the flames flared briefly and subsided.

'My dear Booth! Do come in. It's good of you to spare the time.' With this greeting Dr Mellinger ushered him to a chair beside the fire and proffered his silver cigarette case. 'There's a certain small matter I wanted to discuss, and you are almost the only person who can help me.'

'Of course, Director,' Both assured him. 'I am greatly honoured.'

Dr Mellinger seated himself behind his desk. 'It's a very curious case, one of the most unusual I have ever come across. It concerns a patient under your care, I believe.'

'May I ask for his name, sir?'

'Hinton,' Dr Mellinger said, with a sharp glance at Booth.

'Hinton, sir?'

'You show surprise,' Dr Mellinger continued before Booth could reply. 'I find that response particularly interesting.'

'The search is still being carried on,' Booth said uncertainly as Dr Mellinger paused to digest his remarks. 'I'm afraid we've found absolutely no trace of him. Dr Normand thinks we should inform——'

'Ah, yes, Dr Normand.' The Director revived suddenly. 'I have asked him to report to me with Hinton's file as soon as he is free. Dr Booth, does it occur to you that we may be chasing the wrong hare?'

'Sir——?'

'Is it in fact *Hinton* we are after? I wonder, perhaps, whether the search for Hinton is obscuring something larger and more significant, the enigma, as I mentioned yesterday, which lies at the heart of Green Hill and to whose solution we must all now be dedicated.' Dr Mellinger savoured these reflections before continuing. 'Dr Booth, let us for a moment consider the role of Hinton, or to be more precise, the complex of overlapping and adjacent events that we identify loosely by the term "Hinton".'

'Complex, sir? You speak diagnostically?'

'No, Booth. I am now concerned with the phenomenology of Hinton, with his absolute metaphysical essence. To speak more plainly : has it occurred to you, Booth, how little we know of this elusive patient, how scanty the traces he has left of his own identity?'

'True, Director,' Booth agreed. 'I constantly reproach myself for not taking a closer interest in the patient.'

'Not at all, Doctor. I realize how busy you are. I intend to carry out a major reorganization of Green Hill, and I assure you that your tireless work here will not be forgotten. A senior administrative post would, I am sure, suit you excellently.' As Booth sat up, his interest in the conversation increasing several-fold, Dr Mellinger acknowledged his expression of thanks with a discreet nod. 'As I was saying, Doctor, you have so many patients, all wearing the same uniforms, housed in the same wards, and by and large prescribed the same treatment —is it surprising that they should lose their individual identities? If I may make a small confession,' he added with a roguish smile. 'I myself find that all the patients look alike. Why, if Dr Normand or yourself informed me that a new patient by the name of Smith or Brown had arrived, I would automatically furnish him with the standard uniform of identity at Green Hill—those same lustreless eyes and slack mouth, the same amorphous features.'

Unclasping his hands, Dr Mellinger leaned intently across his desk. 'What I am suggesting, Doctor, is that this automatic mechanism may have operated in the case of the so-called Hinton, and that you may have invested an entirely non-existent individual with the fictions of a personality.'

Dr Booth nodded slowly, 'I see, sir. You suspect that Hinton—or what we have called Hinton up to now— was perhaps a confused memory of another patient.' He hesitated doubtfully, and then noticed that Dr Mellinger's eyes were fixed upon him with hypnotic intensity.

'Dr Booth. I ask you: what actual proof have we that Hinton ever existed?'

'Well, sir, there are the . . .' Booth searched about helplessly . . . 'the records in the administrative department. And the case notes.'

Dr Mellinger shook his head with a scornful flourish. 'My dear Booth, you are speaking of mere pieces of paper. These are not proof of a man's identity. A typewriter will invent anything you choose. The only conclusive proof is his physical existence in time and space or, failing that, a distinct memory of his tangible physical presence. Can you honestly say that either of these conditions is fulfilled?'

'No, sir. I suppose I can't. Though I did speak to a patient whom I assumed to be Hinton.'

'But was he?' The Director's voice was resonant and urgent. 'Search your mind, Booth; be honest with yourself. Was it perhaps another patient to whom you spoke? What doctor ever really looks at his patients? In all probability you merely saw Hinton's name on a list and assumed that he sat before you, an intact physical existence like your own.'

There was a knock upon the door. Dr Normand stepped into the office. 'Good afternoon, Director.'

'Ah, Normand. Do come in. Dr Booth and I have been having a most instructive conversation. I really believe we have found a solution to the mystery of Hinton's disappearance.'

Dr Normand nodded cautiously. 'I am most relieved, sir. I was beginning to wonder whether we should inform the civil authorities. It is now nearly forty-eight hours since . . .'

'My dear Normand, I am afraid you are rather out of touch. Our whole attitude to the Hinton case has changed radically. Dr Booth has been so helpful to me. We have been discussing the possibility that an administrative post might be found for him. You have the Hinton file?'

'Er, I regret not, sir,' Normand apologized, his eyes moving from Booth to the Director. 'I gather it's been temporarily displaced. I've instituted a thorough search and it will be brought to you as soon as possible.'

'Thank you, Normand, if you would.' Mellinger took Booth by the arm and led him to the door. 'Now, Doctor, I am most gratified by your perceptiveness. I want you to question your ward staff in the way I have questioned you. Strike through the mists of illusion and false assumption that swirl about their minds. Warn them of those illusions compounded on illusions which can assume the guise of reality. Remind them, too, that clear minds are required at Green Hill. I will be most surprised if any one of them can put her hand on her heart and swear that Hinton *really* existed.'

After Booth had made his exit, Dr Mellinger returned to his desk. For a moment he failed to notice his deputy.

'Ah, yes, Normand. I wonder where that file is? You didn't bring it?'

'No, sir. As I explained——'

'Well, never mind. But we mustn't become careless, Normand, too much is at stake. Do you realize that without that file we would know literally nothing whatever about Hinton? It would be most awkward.'

'I assure you, sir, the file——'

'Enough, Normand. Don't worry yourself.' Dr Mellinger turned a vulpine smile upon the restless Normand. 'I have the greatest respect for the efficiency of the administrative department under your leadership. I think it unlikely that they should have misplaced it. Tell me, Normand, are you sure that this file ever existed?'

'Certainly, sir,' Normand replied promptly. 'Of course,

I have not actually seen it myself, but every patient at Green Hill has a complete personal file.'

'But Normand,' the Director pointed out gently, 'the patient in question is not *at* Green Hill. Whether or not this hypothetical file exists, Hinton does not.'

He stopped and waited as Normand looked up at him, his eyes narrowing.

A week later, Dr Mellinger held a final conference in his office. This was a notably more relaxed gathering; his subordinates lay back in the leather armchairs around the fire, while Dr Mellinger leaned against the desk, supervising the circulation of his best sherry.

'So, gentlemen,' he remarked in conclusion, 'we may look back on the past week as a period of unique self-discovery, a lesson for all of us to remember the true nature of our roles at Green Hill, our dedication to the task of separating reality from illusion. If our patients are haunted by chimeras, let us at least retain absolute clarity of mind, accepting the validity of any proposition only if all our senses corroborate it. Consider the example of the "Hinton affair". Here, by an accumulation of false assumptions, of illusions buttressing illusions, a vast edifice of fantasy was erected around the wholly mythical identity of one patient. This imaginary figure, who by some means we have not discovered— most probably the error of a typist in the records department—was given the name "Hinton", was subsequently furnished with a complete personal identity, a private ward, attendant nurses and doctors. Such was the grip of this substitute world, this concatenation of errors, that when it crumbled and the lack of any substance behind the shadow was discovered, the remaining vacuum was automatically interpreted as the patient's escape.'

Dr Mellinger gestured eloquently, as Normand, Redpath and Booth nodded their agreement. He walked around his desk and took his seat. 'Perhaps, gentlemen, it is fortunate that I remain aloof from the day-to-day affairs of Green Hill. I take no credit upon myself, that I alone was sufficiently detached to consider the full implications of Hinton's disappearance and realize the only possible explanation—*that Hinton had never existed!*'

'A brilliant deduction,' Redpath murmured.

'Without doubt,' echoed Booth.

'A profound insight,' agreed Normand.

There was a sharp knock on the door. With a frown, Dr Mellinger ignored it and resumed his monologue.

'Thank you, gentlemen. Without your assistance that hypothesis, that Hinton was no more than an accumulation of administrative errors, could never have been confirmed.'

The knock on the door repeated itself. A staff sister appeared breathlessly. 'Excuse me, sir. I'm sorry to interrupt you, but——'

Dr Mellinger waved away her apologies. 'Never mind. What is it?'

'A visitor, Dr Mellinger.' She paused as the Director waited impatiently. 'Mrs Hinton, to see her husband.'

For a moment there was consternation. The three men around the fire sat upright, their drinks forgotten, while Dr Mellinger remained stock-still at his desk. A total silence filled the room, only broken by the light tapping of a woman's heels in the corridor outside.

But Dr Mellinger recovered quickly. Standing up, with a grim smile at his colleagues, he said: 'To see Mr Hinton? Impossible, Hinton never existed. The woman must be suffering from terrible delusions; she requires immediate treatment. Show her in.' He turned to his colleagues. 'Gentlemen, we must do everything we can to help her.'

Minus two.

And baby makes three.

... *Eleven o'clock. Hanson should have reached here by now. Elizabeth! Damn, why does she always move so quietly?*

Climbing down from the window overlooking the road, Freeman ran back to his bed and jumped in, smoothing the blankets over his knees. As his wife poked her head around the door he smiled up at her guilelessly, pretending to read a magazine.

'Everything all right?' she asked, eyeing him shrewdly. She moved her matronly bulk towards him and began to straighten the bed. Freeman fidgeted irritably, pushing her away when she tried to lift him off the pillow on which he was sitting.

'For heaven's sake, Elizabeth, I'm not a child!' he remonstrated, controlling his sing-song voice with difficulty.

'What's happened to Hanson? He was supposed to be here half an hour ago.'

His wife shook her large handsome head and went over to the window. The loose cotton dress disguised her figure, but as she reached up to the bolt Freeman could see the incipient swell of her pregnancy.

'He must have missed his train.' With a single twist of her forearm she securely fastened the upper bolt, which had taken Freeman ten minutes to unlatch.

'I thought I could hear it banging,' she said pointedly. 'We don't want you to catch a cold, do we?'

Freeman waited impatiently for her to leave, glancing at his watch. When his wife paused at the foot of the bed, surveying him carefully, he could barely restrain himself from shouting at her.

'I'm getting the baby's clothes together,' she said, adding aloud to herself, 'which reminds me, you need a new dressing-gown. That old one of yours is losing its shape.'

Freeman pulled the lapels of the dressing-gown across each other, as much to hide his bare chest as to fill out the gown.

'Elizabeth, I've had this for years and it's perfectly good. You're getting an obsession about renewing everything.' He hesitated, realizing the tactlessness of this remark—he should be flattered that she was identifying him with the expected baby. If the strength of the identification was sometimes alarming, this was probably because she was having her first child at a comparatively late age, in her early forties. Besides, he had been ill and bed-ridden during the past month (and what were *his* unconscious motives?) which only served to reinforce the confusion.

'Elizabeth. I'm sorry. It's been good of you to look after me. Perhaps we should call a doctor.'

No! something screamed inside him.

As if hearing this, his wife shook her head in agreement.

'You'll be all right soon. Let nature take its proper course. I don't think you need to see the doctor yet.'

Yet?

Freeman listened to her feet disappearing down the carpeted staircase. A few minutes later the sound of the washing machine drummed out from the kitchen.

Yet!

Freeman slipped quickly out of bed and went into the bathroom.

The cupboard beside the wash-basin was crammed with drying baby clothes, which Elizabeth had either bought or knitted, then carefully washed and sterilized. On each of the five shelves a large square of gauze covered the neat piles, but he could see that most of the clothes were blue, a few white and none pink.

I hope Elizabeth is right, he thought. *If she is it's certainly going to be the world's best-dressed baby. We're supporting an industry single-handed.*

He bent down to the bottom compartment, and from below the tank pulled out a small set of scales. On the shelf immediately above he noticed a large brown garment, a six-year-old's one-piece romper suit. Next to it was a set of vests, outsize, almost big enough to fit Freeman himself. He stripped off his dressing-gown and stepped on to the platform. In the mirror behind the door he examined his small hairless body, with its thin shoulders and narrow hips, long coltish legs.

Six stone nine pounds yesterday. Averting his eyes from the dial, he listened to the washing machine below, then waited for the pointer to steady.

'*Six stone two pounds!*'

Fumbling with his dressing-gown, Freeman pushed the scales under the tank.

Six stone two pounds! A drop of seven pounds in twenty-four hours!

He hurried back into bed, and sat there trembling nervously, fingering for his vanished moustache.

Yet only two months ago he had weighed over eleven stone. Seven pounds in a single day, at this rate——

His mind baulked at the conclusion. Trying to steady his knees, he reached for one of the magazines, turned the pages blindly.

And baby makes two.

He had first become aware of the transformation six weeks earlier, almost immediately after Elizabeth's pregnancy had been confirmed.

Shaving the next morning in the bathroom before going to the office, he discovered that his moustache was thinning. The usually stiff black bristles were soft and flexible, taking on their former ruddy-brown colouring.

His beard, too, was lighter; normally dark and heavy after only a few hours, it yielded before the first few strokes of the razor, leaving his face pink and soft.

Freeman had credited this apparent rejuvenation to the appearance of the baby. He was forty when he married Elizabeth, two or three years her junior, and had assumed unconsciously that he was too old to become a parent, particularly as he had deliberately selected Elizabeth as an ideal mother-substitute, and saw himself as her child rather than as her parental partner. However, now that a child had actually materialized he felt no resentment towards it. Complimenting himself, he decided that he had entered a new phase of maturity and could whole-heartedly throw himself into the role of young parent.

Hence the disappearing moustache, the fading beard, the youthful spring in his step. He crooned:

> 'Just Lizzie and me,
> And baby makes three.'

Behind him, in the mirror, he watched Elizabeth still asleep, her large hips filling the bed. He was glad to see her rest. Contrary to what he had expected, she was even more concerned with him than with the baby, refusing to allow him to prepare his own breakfast. As he brushed his hair, a rich blond growth, sweeping back off his forehead to cover his bald dome, he reflected wryly on the time-honoured saws in the maternity books about the hypersensitivity of expectant fathers—evidently Elizabeth took these counsels seriously.

He tiptoed back into the bedroom and stood by the open window, basking in the crisp early morning air. Downstairs, while he waited for breakfast, he pulled his old tennis racquet out of the hall cupboard, finally woke Elizabeth when one of his practice strokes cracked the glass in the barometer.

To begin with Freeman had revelled in his new-found energy. He took Elizabeth boating, rowing her furiously up and down the river, rediscovering all the physical pleasures he had been too preoccupied to enjoy in his early twenties. He would go shopping with Elizabeth, steering her smoothly along the pavement, carrying all her baby purchases, shoulders back, feeling ten feet tall.

However, it was here that he had his first inkling of what was really happening.

Elizabeth was a large woman, attractive in her way, with broad shoulders and strong hips, and accustomed to wearing high heels. Freeman, a stocky man of medium height, had always been slightly shorter than her, but this had never worried him.

When he found that he barely reached above her shoulder he began to examine himself more closely.

On one of their shopping expeditions (Elizabeth always took Freeman with her, unselfishly asked his opinions, what he preferred, almost as if *he* would be wearing the tiny matinee coats and dresses) a saleswoman unwittingly referred to Elizabeth as his 'mother'. Jolted, Freeman had recognized the obvious disparity between them—the pregnancy was making Elizabeth's face puffy, filling out her neck and shoulders, while his own features were smooth and unlined.

When they reached home he wandered around the lounge and dining-room, realized that the furniture and bookshelves seemed larger and more bulky. Upstairs in the bathroom he climbed on the scales for the first time, found that he had lost one stone six pounds in weight.

Undressing that night, he made another curious discovery.

Elizabeth was taking in the seams of his jackets and trousers. She had said nothing to him about this, and when he saw her sewing away over her needle basket he had assumed she was preparing something for the baby.

During the next days his first flush of spring vigour faded. Strange changes were taking place in his body—his skin and hair, his entire musculature, seemed transformed. The planes of his face had altered, the jaw was trimmer, the nose less prominent, cheeks smooth and unblemished.

Examining his mouth in the mirror, he found that most of his old metal fillings had vanished, firm white enamel taking their place.

He continued to go to the office, conscious of the stares of his colleagues around him. The day after he found he could no longer reach the reference books on the shelf behind his desk he stayed at home, feigning an attack of influenza.

Elizabeth seemed to understand completely. Freeman had said nothing to her, afraid that she might be terrified into a miscarriage if she learned the truth. Swathed in his old dressing-gown, a woollen scarf around his neck and chest to make his slim figure appear more bulky, he sat on the sofa in the lounge, blankets piled across him, a firm cushion raising him higher off the seat.

Carefully he tried to avoid standing whenever Elizabeth was in the room, and when absolutely necessary circled behind the furniture on tiptoe.

A week later, however, when his feet no longer touched the floor below the dining-room table, he decided to remain in his bed upstairs.

Elizabeth agreed readily. All the while she watched her husband with her bland impassive eyes, quietly readying herself for the baby.

Damn Hanson, Freeman thought. At eleven forty-five he had still not appeared. Freeman flipped through the magazine without looking at it, glancing irritably at his watch every few seconds. The strap was now too large for his wrist and twice he had prised additional holes for the clasp.

How to describe his metamorphosis to Hanson he had not decided, plagued as he was by curious doubts. He was not even sure what *was* happening. Certainly he had lost a remarkable amount of weight—up to eight or nine pounds each day—and almost a foot in height, but without any accompanying loss of health. He had, in fact, reverted to the age and physique of a fourteen-year-old schoolboy.

But what was the real explanation? Freeman asked himself. Was the rejuvenation some sort of psychosomatic excess? Although he felt no conscious animosity towards the expected baby, was he in the grip of an insane attempt at retaliation?

It was this possibility, with its logical prospect of padded cells and white-coated guards, that had frightened Freeman into silence. Elizabeth's doctor was brusque and unsympathetic, and almost certainly would regard Freeman as a neurotic malingerer, perpetrating an elaborate charade designed to substitute himself for his own child in his wife's affections.

Also, Freeman knew, there were other motives, obscure and intangible. Frightened of examining them, he began to read the magazine.

It was a schoolchild's comic. Annoyed, Freeman stared at the cover, then looked at the stack of magazines which Elizabeth had ordered from the newsagent that morning. They were all the same.

His wife entered her bedroom on the other side of the landing. Freeman slept alone now in what would eventually be the baby's nursery, partly to give himself enough privacy to think, and also to save him the embarrassment of revealing his shrinking body to his wife.

She came in, carrying a small tray on which were a glass of warm milk and two biscuits, Although he was losing weight, Freeman had the eager appetite of a child. He took the biscuits and ate them hurriedly.

Elizabeth sat on the bed, producing a brochure from the pocket of her apron.

'I want to order the baby's cot,' she told him. 'Would you like to choose one of the designs?'

Freeman waved airily. 'Any of them will do. Pick one that's strong and heavy, something he won't be able to climb out of too easily.'

His wife nodded, watching him pensively. All afternoon she spent ironing and cleaning, moving the piles of dry linen into the cupboards on the landing, disinfecting pails and buckets.

They had decided she would have the baby at home.

Four and a half stone!

Freeman gasped at the dial below his feet. During the previous two days he had lost over one stone six pounds, had barely been able to reach up to the handle of the cupboard and open the door. Trying not to look at himself in the mirror, he realized he was now the size of a six-year-old, with a slim chest, slender neck and face. The skirt of the dressing-gown trailed across the floor behind him, and only with difficulty could he keep his arms through the voluminous sleeves.

When Elizabeth came up with his breakfast she examined him critically, put the tray down and went out to one of the landing cupboards. She returned with a small sports-shirt and a pair of corduroy shorts.

'Would you like to wear these, dear?' she asked. 'You'll find them more comfortable.'

Reluctant to use his voice, which had degenerated into a piping treble, Freeman shook his head. After she had gone, however, he pulled off the heavy dressing-gown and put on the garments.

Suppressing his doubts, he wondered how to reach the doctor without having to go downstairs to the telephone. So far he had managed to avoid raising his wife's suspicions, but now there was no hope of continuing to do so. He barely reached up to her waist. If she saw him standing upright she might well die of shock on the spot.

Fortunately, Elizabeth left him alone. Once, just after lunch, two men arrived in a van from the department store and delivered a blue cot and play-pen, but he pretended to be asleep until they had gone. Despite his anxiety, Freeman easily fell asleep—he had begun to feel tired after lunch—and woke two hours later to find that Elizabeth had made the bed in the cot, swathing the blue blankets and pillow in a plastic sheet.

Below this, shackled to the wooden sides, he could see the white leather straps of a restraining harness.

The next morning Freeman decided to escape. His weight was down to only three stone one pound, and the clothes Elizabeth had given him the previous day were already three sizes too large, the trousers supporting themselves precariously around his slender waist. In the bathroom mirror Freeman stared at the small boy, watching him with wide eyes. Dimly he remembered snapshots of his own childhood.

After breakfast, when Elizabeth was out in the garden, he crept downstairs. Through the window he saw her open the dustbin and push inside his business suit and black leather shoes.

Freeman waited helplessly for a moment, and then hurried back to his room. Striding up the huge steps required more effort than he imagined, and by the time he reached the top flight he was too exhausted to climb on to the bed. Panting, he leaned against it for a few minutes. Even if he reached the hospital, how could he convince anyone there of what had happened without having to call Elizabeth along to identify him?

Fortunately, his intelligence was still intact. Given a pencil and paper he would soon demonstrate his adult mind, a circumstantial knowledge of social affairs that no infant prodigy could ever possess.

His first task was to reach the hospital or, failing that, the local police station. Luckily, all he needed to do was walk along the nearest main thoroughfare—a four-year-old child wandering about on his own would soon be picked up by a constable on duty.

Below, he heard Elizabeth come slowly up the stairs, the laundry basket creaking under her arm. Freeman tried to lift himself on to the bed, but only succeeded in disarranging the sheets. As Elizabeth opened the door he ran around to the far side of the bed and hid his tiny body behind it, resting his chin on the bedspread.

Elizabeth paused, watching his small plump face. For a moment they gazed at each other, Freeman's heart pounding, wondering how she could fail to realize what had happened to him. But she merely smiled and walked through into the bathroom.

Supporting himself on the bedside table, he climbed in, his face away from the bathroom door. On her way out Elizabeth bent down and tucked him up, then slipped out of the room, shutting the door behind her.

The rest of the day Freeman waited for an opportunity to escape, but his wife was busy upstairs, and early that evening, before he could prevent himself, he fell into a deep dreamless sleep.

He woke in a vast white room. Blue light dappled the high walls, along which a line of giant animal figures danced and gambolled. Looking around, he realized that he was still in the nursery. He was wearing a small pair of polka-dot pyjamas (had Elizabeth changed him while he slept?) but they were almost too large for his shrunken arms and legs.

A miniature dressing-gown had been laid out across the foot of the bed, a pair of slippers on the floor. Freeman climbed down from the bed and put them on, his balance unsteady. The door was closed, but he pulled a chair over and stood on it, turning the handle with his two small fists.

On the landing he paused, listening carefully. Elizabeth was in the kitchen, humming to herself. One step at a time, Freeman moved down the staircase, watching his wife through the rail. She was standing over the cooker, her broad back almost hiding the machine, warming some milk gruel. Freeman waited until she turned to the sink, then ran across the hall into the lounge and out through the french windows.

The thick soles of his carpet slippers muffled his footsteps, and he broke into a run once he reached the shelter of the front garden. The gate was almost too stiff for him to open, and as he fumbled with the latch a middle-aged woman stopped and peered down at him, frowning at the windows.

Freeman pretended to run back into the house, hoping that Elizabeth had not yet discovered his disappearance. When the woman moved off, he opened the gate, and hurried down the street towards the shopping centre.

He had entered an enormous world. The two-storey houses loomed like canyon walls, the end of the street one hundred yards away below the horizon. The paving stones were massive and uneven, the tall sycamores as distant as the sky. A car came towards him, daylight between its wheels, hesitated and sped on.

He was still fifty yards from the corner when he tripped over one of the pavement stones and was forced to stop. Out of breath, he leaned against a tree, his legs exhausted.

He heard a gate open, and over his shoulder saw Elizabeth glance up and down the street. Quickly he stepped behind the tree, waited until she returned to the house, and then set off again.

Suddenly, sweeping down from the sky, a vast arm lifted him off his feet. Gasping with surprise, he looked up into the face of Mr Symonds, his bank manager.

'You're out early, young man,' Symonds said. He put Freeman down, holding him tightly by one hand. His car was parked in the drive next to them. Leaving the engine running, he began to walk Freeman back down the street. 'Now, let's see, where do you live?'

Freeman tried to pull himself away, jerking his arm furiously, but Symonds hardly noticed his efforts. Elizabeth stepped out of the gate, an apron around her waist, and hurried towards them. Freeman tried to hide between Symond's legs, felt himself picked up in the bank manager's strong arms and handed to Elizabeth. She held him firmly, his head over her broad shoulder, thanked Symonds and carried him back into the house.

As they crossed the pathway Freeman hung limply, trying to will himself out of existence.

In the nursery he waited for his feet to touch the bed, ready to dive below the blankets, but instead Elizabeth lowered him carefully to the floor, and he discovered he had been placed in the baby's play-pen. He held the rail uncertainly, while Elizabeth bent over and straightened his dressing-gown. Then, to Freeman's relief, she turned away.

For five minutes Freeman stood numbly by the rail, outwardly recovering his breath, but at the same time gradually realizing something of which he had been dimly afraid for several days—by an extraordinary inversion of logic, Elizabeth identified him with the baby inside her womb! Far from showing surprise at Freeman's transformation into a three-year-old child, his wife merely accepted this as a natural concomitant of her own pregnancy. In her mind she had externalized the child within her. As Freeman shrank progressively smaller, mirroring the growth of her child, her eyes were fixed on their common focus, and all she could see was the image of her baby.

Still searching for a means of escape, Freeman discovered that he was unable to climb out of the play-pen. The light wooden bars were too strong for his small arms to break, the whole cage too heavy to lift. Exhausting himself, he sat down on the floor, and fiddled nervously with a large coloured ball.

Instead of trying to evade Elizabeth and hide his transformation from her, he realized that he must now attract her attention and force her to recognize his real identity.

Standing up, he began to rock the play-pen from side to side, edging it across to the wall where the sharp corner set up a steady battering.

Elizabeth came out of her bedroom.

'Now, darling, what's all the noise for?' she asked, smiling at him. 'How about a biscuit?' She knelt down by the pen, her face only a few inches from Freeman's.

Screwing up his courage, Freeman looked straight at her, searching the large, unblinking eyes. He took the biscuit, cleared his throat and said carefully: 'I'd nod blor aby.'

Elizabeth ruffled his long blond hair. 'Aren't you, darling? What a sad shame.'

Freeman stamped his foot, then flexed his lips. 'I'd nod blor aby!' he shouted. 'I'd blor usban!'

Laughing to herself, Elizabeth began to empty the wardrobe beside the bed. As Freeman remonstrated with her, struggling helplessly with the strings of consonants, she took out his dinner jacket and overcoat. Then she emptied the chest of drawers, lifting out his shirts and socks, and wrapped them away inside a sheet.

After she had carried everything out she returned and stripped the bed, pushed it back against the wall, putting the baby cot in its place.

Clutching the rail of the play-pen, Freeman watched dumbfounded as the last remnants of his former existence were dispatched below.

'Lisbeg, lep me, I'd——!'

He gave up, searched the floor of the play-pen for something to write with. Summoning his energies, he rocked the cot over to the wall, and in large letters, using the spit which flowed amply from his mouth, wrote:

ELIZABETH HELP ME! I AM NOT A BABY

Banging on the door with his fists, he finally attracted Elizabeth's attention, but when he pointed to the wall the marks had dried. Weeping with frustration, Freeman toddled across the cage and began to retrace the message. Before he had completed more than two or three letters Elizabeth put her arms around his waist and lifted him out.

A single place had been set at the head of the dining-room table, a new high chair beside it. Still trying to form a coherent sentence, Freeman felt himself rammed into the seat, a large bib tied around his neck.

During the meal he watched Elizabeth carefully, hoping to detect in her motionless face some inkling of recognition, even a fleeting awareness that the two-year-old child sitting in front of her was her husband. Freeman played with his food, smearing crude messages on the tray around his dish, but when he pointed at them Elizabeth clapped her hands, apparently joining in his little triumphs, and then wiped the tray clean. Worn out, Freeman let himself be carried upstairs, lay strapped in the cot under the miniature blankets.

Time was against him. By now, he found, he was

asleep for the greater portion of each day. For the first
hours he felt fresh and alert, but his energy faded rapidly
and after each meal an overwhelming lethargy closed his
eyes like a sleeping draught. Dimly he was aware that
his metamorphosis continued unchecked—when he
woke he could sit up only with difficulty. The effort of
standing upright on his buckling legs tired him after a
few minutes.

His power of speech had vanished. All he could pro-
duce were a few grotesque grunts, or an inarticulate
babble. Lying on his back with a bottle of hot milk in his
mouth, he knew that his one hope was Hanson. Sooner
or later he would call in and discover that Freeman had
disappeared and all traces of him had been carefully
removed.

Propped against a cushion on the carpet in the lounge,
Freeman noted that Elizabeth had emptied his desk and
taken down his books from the shelves beside the fire-
place. To all intents she was now the widowed mother
of a twelve-month old son, parted from her husband
since their honeymoon.

Unconsciously she had begun to assume this role.
When they went out for their morning walks, Freeman
strapped back into the pram, a celluloid rabbit rattling a
few inches from his nose and almost driving him insane,
they passed many people he had known by sight, and all
took it for granted that he was Elizabeth's son. As they
bent over the pram, poking him in the stomach and
complimenting Elizabeth on his size and precosity,
several of them referred to her husband, and Elizabeth
replied that he was away on an extended trip. In her
mind, obviously, she had already dismissed Freeman,
forgetting that he had ever existed.

He realized how wrong he was when they returned from
what was to be his last outing.

As they neared home Elizabeth hesitated slightly, jolting the pram, apparently uncertain whether to retrace her steps. Someone shouted at them from the distance, and as Freeman tried to identify the familiar voice Elizabeth bent forwards and pulled the hood over his head.

Struggling to free himself, Freeman recognized the tall figure of Hanson towering over the pram, doffing his hat.

'Mrs Freeman, I've been trying to ring you all week. How are you?'

'Very well, Mr Hanson.' She jerked the pram around, trying to keep it between herself and Hanson. Freeman could see that she was momentarily confused. 'I'm afraid our telephone is out of order.'

Hanson side-stepped around the pram, watching Elizabeth with interest. 'What happened to Charles on Saturday? Have to go off on business?'

Elizabeth nodded. 'He was very sorry, Mr Hanson, but something important came up. He'll be away for some time.'

She knew, Freeman said automatically to himself.

Hanson peered under the hood at Freeman. 'Out for a morning stroll, little chap?' To Elizabeth he commented: 'Fine baby there. I always like the angry-looking ones. Your neighbour's?'

Elizabeth shook her head. 'The son of a friend of Charles's. We must be getting along, Mr Hanson.'

'Do call me Robert. See you again soon, eh?'

Elizabeth smiled, her face composed again. 'I'm sure we will, Robert.'

'Good show.' With a roguish grin, Hanson walked off.

She knew!

Astounded, Freeman pushed the blankets back as far as he could, watching Hanson's retreating figure. He turned once to wave to Elizabeth, who raised her hand

and then steered the pram through the gate.

Freeman tried to sit up, his eyes fixed on Elizabeth, hoping she would see the anger in his face. But she wheeled the pram swiftly into the passage-way, un-unfastened the straps and lifted Freeman out.

As they went up the staircase he looked down over her shoulder at the telephone, saw that the receiver was off its cradle. All along she had known what was happening, had deliberately pretended not to notice his metamorphosis. She had anticipated each stage of the transformation, the comprehensive wardrobe had been purchased well in advance, the succession of smaller and smaller garments, the play-pen and cot, had been ordered for him, not for the baby.

For a moment Freeman wondered whether she was pregnant at all. The facial puffiness, the broadening figure, might well have been illusory. When she told him she was expecting a baby he had never imagined that *he* would be the baby.

Handling him roughly, she bundled Freeman into his cot and secured him under the blankets. Downstairs he could hear her moving about rapidly, apparently preparing for some emergency. Propelled by an uncharacteristic urgency, she was closing the windows and doors. As he listened to her, Freeman noticed how cold he felt. His small body was swaddled like a new-born infant in a mass of shawls, but his bones were like sticks of ice. A curious drowsiness was coming over him, draining away his anger and fear, and the centre of his awareness was shifting from his eyes to his skin. The thin afternoon light stung his eyes, and as they closed he slipped off into a blurring limbo of shallow sleep, the tender surface of his body aching for relief.

Some while later he felt Elizabeth's hands pull away the blankets, and was aware of her carrying him across the hallway. Gradually his memory of the house and his own identity began to fade, and his shrinking body clung helplessly to Elizabeth as she lay on her broad bed.

Hating the naked hair that rasped across his face, he now felt clearly for the first time what he had for so long repressed. Before the end he cried out suddenly with joy and wonder, as he remembered the drowned world of his first childhood.

As the child within her quietened, stirring for the last time, Elizabeth sank back on to the pillow, the birth pains slowly receding. Gradually she felt her strength return, the vast world within her settling and annealing itself. Staring at the darkened ceiling, she lay resting for several hours, now and then adjusting her large figure to fit the unfamiliar contours of the bed.

The next morning she rose for half an hour. The child already seemed less burdensome, and three days later she was able to leave her bed completely, a loose smock hiding what remained of her pregnancy. Immediately she began the last task, clearing away all that remained of the baby's clothing, dismantling the cot and play-pen. The clothing she tied into large parcels, then telephoned a local charity which came and collected them. The pram and cot she sold to the second-hand dealer who drove down the street. Within two days she had erased every trace of her husband, stripping the coloured illustrations from the nursery walls and replacing the spare bed in the centre of the floor.

All that remained was the diminishing knot within her, a small clenching fist. When she could almost no longer feel it Elizabeth went to her jewel box and took off her wedding ring.

On her return from the shopping centre the next morning, Elizabeth noticed someone hailing her from a car parked outside her gate.

'Mrs Freeman!' Hanson jumped out of the car and accosted her gaily. 'It's wonderful to see you looking so well.'

Elizabeth gave him a wide heart-warming smile, her handsome face made more sensual by the tumescence of her features. She was wearing a bright silk dress and all visible traces of the pregnancy had vanished.

'Where's Charles?' Hanson asked. 'Still away?'

Elizabeth's smile broadened, her lips parted across her strong white teeth. Her face was curiously expressionless, her eyes momentarily fixed on some horizon far beyond Hanson's face.

Hanson waited uncertainly for Elizabeth to reply. Then, taking the hint, he leaned back into his car and switched off the engine. He rejoined Elizabeth, holding the gate open for her.

So Elizabeth met her husband. Three hours later the metamorphosis of Charles Freeman reached its climax. In that last second Freeman came to his true beginning, the moment of his conception coinciding with the moment of his extinction, the end of his last birth with the beginning of his first death.

And baby makes one.

Larsen had been waiting all day for Bayliss, the psychologist who lived in the next chalet, to pay the call he had promised on the previous evening. Characteristically, Bayliss had made no precise arrangements as regards time; a tall, moody man with an off-hand manner, he had merely gestured vaguely with his hypodermic and mumbled something about the following day: he would look in, probably. Larsen knew damned well he would look in, the case was too interesting to miss. In an oblique way it meant as much to Bayliss as it did to himself.

Except that it was Larsen who had to do the worrying—by three that afternoon Bayliss had still not materialized. What was he doing except sitting in his white-walled, air-conditioned lounge, playing Bartok quartets on the stereogram? Meanwhile Larsen had nothing to do but roam around the chalet, slamming impatiently from one room to the next like a tiger with an anxiety neurosis, and cook up a quick lunch (coffee and three amphetamines, from a private cache Bayliss as yet only dimly suspected. God, he needed the stimulants after those massive barbiturate shots Bayliss had pumped into him after the attack). He tried to settle down with Kretschmer's *An Analysis of Psychotic Time*, a heavy tome, full of graphs and tabular material, which Bayliss had insisted he read, asserting that it filled in necessary background to the case. Larsen had spent a couple of hours on it, but so far he had got no further than the preface to the third edition.

Periodically he went over to the window and peered through the plastic blind for any signs of movement in the next chalet. Beyond, the desert lay in the sunlight like an enormous bone, against which the aztec-red fins of Bayliss's Pontiac flared like the tail feathers of a flamboyant phoenix. The remaining three chalets were empty; the complex was operated by the electronics company for which he and Bayliss worked as a sort of 're-creational' centre for senior executives and tired 'think-men'. The desert site had been chosen for its hypotensive virtues, its supposed equivalence to psychic zero. Two or three days of leisurely reading, of watching the motionless horizon, and tension and anxiety thresholds rose to more useful levels.

However, two days there, Larsen reflected, and he had very nearly gone mad. It was lucky Bayliss had been around with his hypodermic. Though the man was certainly casual when it came to supervising his patients; he left them to their own resources. In fact, looking back, he—Larsen—had been responsible for just about all the diagnosis. Bayliss had done little more than thumb his hypo, toss Kretschmer into his lap, and offer some cogitating asides.

Perhaps he was waiting for something?

Larsen tried to decide whether to phone Bayliss on some pretext; his number—O, on the internal system—was almost too inviting. Then he heard a door clatter outside, and saw the tall, angular figure of the psychologist crossing the concrete apron between the chalets, head bowed pensively in the sharp sunlight.

Where's his case, Larsen throught, almost disappointed. Don't tell me he's putting on the barbiturate brakes. Maybe he'll try hypnosis. Masses of post-hypnotic suggestions, in the middle of shaving I'll suddenly stand on my head.

He let Bayliss in, fidgeting around him as they went into the lounge.

'Where the hell have you been?' he asked. 'Do you realize it's nearly four?'

Bayliss sat down at the miniature executive desk in the middle of the lounge and looked round critically, a ploy Larsen resented but never managed to anticipate.

'Of course I realize it. I'm fully wired for time. How have you felt today?' He pointed to the straight-backed chair placed in the interviewee's position. 'Sit down and try to relax.'

Larsen gestured irritably. 'How can I relax while I'm just hanging around here, waiting for the next bomb to go off?' He began his analysis of the past twenty-four hours, a task he enjoyed, larding the case history with liberal doses of speculative commentary.

'Actually, last night was easier. I think I'm entering a new zone. Everything's beginning to stabilize, I'm not looking over my shoulder all the time. I've left the inside doors open, and before I enter a room I deliberately anticipate it, try to extrapolate its depth and dimensions so that it doesn't *surprise* me—before I used to open a door and just dive through like a man stepping into an empty lift shaft.'

Larsen paced up and down, cracking his knuckles. Eyes half closed, Bayliss watched him. 'I'm pretty sure there won't be another attack,' Larsen continued. 'In fact, the best thing is probably for me to get straight back to the plant. After all, there's no point in sitting around here indefinitely. I feel more or less completely okay.'

Bayliss nodded. 'In that case, then, why are you so jumpy?'

Exasperated, Larsen clenched his fists. He could almost hear the artery thudding in his temple. 'I'm *not* jumpy! For God's sake, Bayliss, I thought the advanced view was that psychiatrist and patient shared the illness together, forgot their own identities and took equal responsibility. You're trying to evade——'

'I am not,' Bayliss cut in firmly. 'I accept complete responsibility for you. That's why I want you to stay here until you've come to terms with this thing.'

Larsen snorted. ' "Thing"! Now you're trying to make it sound like something out of a horror film. All I had was a simple hallucination. And I'm not even completely convinced it was that.' He pointed through the window. 'Suddenly opening the garage door in that bright sunlight—it might have been a shadow.'

'You described it pretty exactly,' Bayliss commented. 'Colour of the hair, moustache, the clothes he wore.'

'Back projection. The detail in dreams is authentic too.' Larsen moved the chair out of the way and leaned forwards across the desk. 'Another thing. I don't feel you're being entirely frank.'

Their eyes levelled. Bayliss studied Larsen carefully for a moment, noticing his widely dilated pupils.

'Well?' Larsen pressed.

Bayliss buttoned his jacket and walked across to the door. 'I'll call in tomorrow. Meanwhile try to unwind yourself a little. I'm not trying to alarm you, Larsen, but this problem may be rather more complicated than you imagine.' He nodded, then slipped out before Larsen could reply.

Larsen stepped over to the window and through the blind watched the psychologist disappear into his chalet. Disturbed for a moment, the sunlight again settled itself heavily over everything. A few minutes later the sounds of one of the Bartok quartets whined fretfully across the apron.

Larsen went back to the desk and sat down, elbows thrust forwards aggressively. Bayliss irritated him, with his neurotic music and inaccurate diagnoses. He felt tempted to climb straight into his car and drive back to the plant. Strictly speaking, though, the psychologist outranked Larsen, and probably had executive authority over him while he was at the chalet, particularly as the five days he had spent there were on the company's time.

He gazed round the silent lounge, tracing the cool horizontal shadows that dappled the walls, listening to the low soothing hum of the air-conditioner. His argument with Bayliss had refreshed him and he felt composed and confident. Yet residues of tension and uneasiness still existed, and he found it difficult to keep his eyes off the open doors to the bedroom and kitchen.

He had arrived at the chalet five days earlier, exhausted and overwrought, on the verge of a total nervous collapse. For three months he had been working without a break on programming the complex circuitry of a huge brain simulator which the company's Advanced Designs Division were building for one of the major psychiatric foundations. This was a complete electronic replica of the central nervous system, each spinal level represented by a single computer, other computers holding memory banks in which sleep, tension, aggression and other psychic functions were coded and stored, building blocks that could be played into the C.N.S. simulator to construct models of dissociation states and withdrawal syndromes—any psychic complex on demand.

The design teams working on the simulator had been watched vigilantly by Bayliss and his assistants, and the weekly tests had revealed the mounting load of fatigue that Larsen was carrying. Finally Bayliss had pulled him off the project and sent him out to the desert for two or three days' recuperation.

Larsen had been glad to get away. For the first two days he had lounged aimlessly around the deserted chalets, pleasantly fuddled by the barbiturates Bayliss prescribed, gazing out across the white deck of the desert floor, going to bed by eight and sleeping until noon. Every morning the caretaker had driven in from the town near by to clean up and leave the groceries and menu slips, but Larsen never saw her. He was only too glad to be alone. Deliberately seeing no one, allowing the natural rhythms of his mind to re-establish themselves, he knew he would soon recover.

In fact, however, the first person he had seen had stepped up to him straight out of a nightmare.

Larsen still looked back on the encounter with a shudder.

After lunch on his third day at the chalet he had decided to drive out into the desert and examine an old quartz mine in one of the canyons. This was a two-hour trip and he had made up a thermos of iced martini. The garage was adjacent to the chalet, set back from the kitchen side entrance, and fitted with a roll steel door that lifted vertically and curved up under the roof.

Larsen had locked the chalet behind him, then raised the garage door and driven his car out on to the apron. Going back for the thermos which he had left on the bench at the rear of the garage, he had noticed a full can of petrol in the shadows against one corner. For a moment he paused, adding up his mileage, and decided to take the can with him. He carried it over to the car, then turned round to close the garage door.

The roll had failed to retreat completely when he had first raised it, and reached down to the level of his chin. Putting his weight on the handle, Larsen managed to move it down a few inches, but the inertia was too much for him. The sunlight reflected in the steel panels was dazzling his eyes. Pressing his palms under the door, he jerked it upwards slightly to gain more momentum on the downward swing.

The space was small, no more than six inches, but it was just enough for him to see into the darkened garage.

Hiding in the shadows against the back wall near the bench was the indistinct but nonetheless unmistakable figure of a man. He stood motionless, arms loosely at his sides, watching Larsen. He wore a light cream suit—

covered by patches of shadow that gave him a curious fragmentary look—a neat blue sports-shirt and two-tone shoes. He was stockily built, with a thick brush.moustache, a plump face, and eyes that stared steadily at Larsen but somehow seemed to be focused beyond him.

Still holding the door with both hands, Larsen gaped at the man. Not only was there no means by which he could have entered the garage—there were no windows or side doors—but there was something aggressive about his stance.

Larsen was about to call to him when the man moved forward and stepped straight out of the shadows towards him.

Aghast, Larsen backed away. The dark patches across the man's suit were not shadows at all, but the outline of the work bench directly behind him.

The man's body and clothes were transparent.

Galvanized into life, Larsen seized the garage door and hurled it down. He snapped the bolt in and jammed it closed with both hands, knees pressed against it.

Half paralysed by cramp and barely breathing, his suit soaked with sweat, he was still holding the door down when Bayliss drove up thirty minutes later.

Larsen drummed his fingers irritably on the desk, stood up and went into the kitchen. Cut off from the barbiturates they had been intended to counteract, the three amphetamines had begun to make him feel restless and overstimulated. He switched the coffee percolator on and then off, prowled back to the lounge and sat down on the sofa with the copy of Kretschmer.

He read a few pages, increasingly impatient. What light Kretschmer threw on his problem was hard to see; most of the case histories described deep schizos and irreversible paranoids. His own problem was much more superficial, a momentary aberration due to overloading.

Why wouldn't Bayliss see this? For some reason he seemed to be unconsciously wishing for a major crisis, probably because he, the psychologist, secretly wanted to become the patient.

Larsen tossed the book aside and looked out through the window at the desert. Suddenly the chalet seemed dark and cramped, a claustrophobic focus of suppressed aggressions. He stood up, strode over to the door and stepped out into the clear open air.

Grouped in a loose semicircle, the chalets seemed to shrink towards the ground as he strolled to the rim of the concrete apron a hundred yards away. The mountains behind loomed up enormously. It was late afternoon, on the edge of dusk, and the sky was a vivid vibrant blue, the deepening colours of the desert floor overlaid by the huge lanes of shadow that reached from the mountains against the sunline. Larsen looked back at the chalets. There was no sign of movement, other than a faint discordant echo of the atonal music Bayliss was playing. The whole scene seemed suddenly unreal.

Reflecting on this, Larsen felt something shift inside his mind. The sensation was undefined, like an expected cue that had failed to materialize, a forgotten intention. He tried to recall it, unable to remember whether he had switched on the coffee percolator.

He walked back to the chalets, noticing that he had left the kitchen door open. As he passed the lounge window on his way to close it he glanced in.

A man was sitting on the sofa, legs crossed, face hidden by the volume of Kretschmer. For a moment Larsen assumed that Bayliss had called in to see him, and walked on, deciding to make coffee for them both. Then he noticed that the stereogram was still playing in Bayliss's chalet.

Picking his steps carefully, he moved back to the lounge window. The man's face was still hidden, but a single glance confirmed that the visitor was not Bayliss. He was wearing the same cream suit Larsen had seen two days earlier, the same two-tone shoes. But this time the man was no hallucination; his hands and clothes were solid and palpable. He shifted about on the sofa, denting one of the cushions, and turned a page of the book, flexing the spine between his hands.

Pulse thickening, Larsen braced himself against the window-ledge. Something about the man, his posture, the way he held his hands, convinced him that he had seen him before their fragmentary encounter in the garage.

Then the man lowered the book and threw it on to the seat beside him. He sat back and looked through the window, his focus only a few inches from Larsen's face.

Mesmerized, Larsen stared back at him. He recognized the man without doubt, the pudgy face, the nervous eyes, the too thick moustache. Now at last he could see him clearly and realized he knew him only too well, better than anyone else on Earth.

The man was himself.

Bayliss clipped the hypodermic into his valise, and placed it on the lid of the stereogram.

'Hallucination is the wrong term altogether,' he told Larsen, who was lying stretched out on Bayliss's sofa, sipping weakly at a glass of hot whisky. 'Stop using it. A psychoretinal image of remarkable strength and duration, but not an hallucination.'

Larsen gestured feebly. He had stumbled into Bayliss's chalet an hour earlier, literally beside himself with fright. Bayliss had calmed him down, then dragged him back across the apron to the lounge window and made him accept that his double was gone. Bayliss was not in the least surprised at the identity of the phantom, and this worried Larsen almost as much as the actual hallucination. What else was Bayliss hiding up his sleeve?

'I'm surprised you didn't realize it sooner yourself,' Bayliss remarked. 'Your description of the man in the garage was so obvious—the same cream suit, the same shoes and shirt, let alone the exact physical similarity, even down to your moustache.'

Recovering a little, Larsen sat up. He smoothed down his cream gabardine suit and brushed the dust off his brown-and-white shoes. 'Thanks for warning me. All you've got to do now is tell me who he is.'

Bayliss sat down in one of the chairs. 'What do you mean, who he is? He's you, of course.'

'I know that, but why, where does he come from? God, I must be going insane.'

Bayliss snapped his fingers. 'No you're not. Pull yourself together. This is a purely functional disorder, like double vision or amnesia; nothing more serious. If it was, I'd have pulled you out of here long ago. Perhaps I should have done that anyway, but I think we can find a safe way out of the maze you're in.'

He took a notebook out of his breast pocket. 'Let's have a look at what we've got. Now, two features stand out. First, the phantom is yourself. There's no doubt about that; he's an exact replica of you. More important, though, he is you as you are now, your exact contemporary in time, unidealized and unmutilated. He isn't the shining hero of the super-ego, or the haggard greybeard of the death wish. He is simply a photographic double. Displace one eyeball with your finger and you'll see a double of me. Your double is no more unusual, with the exception that the displacement is not in space but in time. You see, the second thing I noticed about your garbled description of this phantom was that, not only was he a photographic double, but he was doing exactly what you yourself had been doing a few minutes previously. The man in the garage was standing by the workbench, just where you stood when you were wondering whether to take the can of petrol. Again, the man reading in the armchair was merely repeating exactly what you had been doing with the same book five minutes earlier. He even stared out of the window as you say you did before going out for a stroll.'

Larsen nodded, sipping his whisky. 'You're suggesting that the hallucination was a mental flashback?'

'Precisely. The stream of retinal images reaching the optic lobe is nothing more than a film strip. Every image is stored away, thousands of reels, a hundred thousand hours of running time. Usually flashbacks are deliberate, when we consciously select a few blurry stills from the film library, a childhood scene, the image of our neighbourhood streets we carry around with us all day near the surface of consciousness. But upset the projector slightly—overstrain could do it—jolt it back a few hundred frames, and you'll superimpose a completely irrelevant strip of already exposed film, in your case a glimpse of yourself sitting on the sofa. It's the apparent irrelevancy that is so frightening.'

Larsen gestured with his glass. 'Wait a minute, though. When I was sitting on the sofa reading Kretschmer I didn't actually see myself, any more than I can see myself now. So where did the superimposed images come from?'

Bayliss put away his notebook. 'Don't take the analogy of the film strip too literally. You may not see yourself sitting on that sofa, but your awareness of being there is just as powerful as any visual corroboration. It's the stream of tactile, positional and psychic images that form the real data store. Very little extrapolation is needed to transpose the observer's eye a few yards to the other side of a room. Purely visual memories are never completely accurate anyway.'

'How do you explain why the man I saw in the garage

was transparent?'

'Quite simply. The process was only just beginning, the intensity of the image was weak. The one you saw this afternoon was much stronger. I cut you off barbiturates deliberately, knowing full well that those stimulants you were taking on the sly would set off something if they were allowed to operate unopposed.'

He went over to Larsen, took his glass and refilled it from the decanter. 'But let's think of the future. The most interesting aspect of all this is the light it throws on one of the oldest archetypes of the human psyche—the ghost—and the whole supernatural army of phantoms, witches, demons and so on. Are they all, in fact, nothing more than psychoretinal flashbacks, transposed images of the observer himself, jolted on to the retinal screen by fear, bereavement, religious obsession? The most notable thing about the majority of ghosts is how prosaically equipped they are, compared with the elaborate literary productions of the great mystics and dreamers. The nebulous white sheet is probably the observer's own nightgown. It's an interesting field for speculation. For example, take the most famous ghost in literature and reflect how much more sense Hamlet makes if you realize that the ghost of his murdered father is really Hamlet himself.'

'All right, all right,' Larsen cut in irritably. 'But how does this help me?'

Bayliss broke off his reflective up-and-down patrol of the floor and fixed an eye on Larsen. 'I'm coming to that. There are two methods of dealing with this disfunction of yours. The classical technique is to pump you full of tranquillizers and confine you to a bed for a year or so. Gradually your mind would knit together. Long job, boring for you and everybody else. The alternative method is, frankly, experimental, but I think it might work. I mentioned the phenomenon of the ghost because it's an interesting fact that although there have been tens of thousands of recorded cases of people being pursued by ghosts, and a few of the ghosts themselves being pursued, there have been no cases of ghost and observer actually meeting of their own volition. Tell me, what would have happened if, when you saw your double this afternoon, you had gone straight into the lounge and spoken to him?'

Larsen shuddered. 'Obviously nothing, if your theory holds. I wouldn't like to test it.'

'That's just what you're going to do. Don't panic. The next time you see a double sitting in a chair reading Kretschmer, go up and speak to him. If he doesn't reply sit down in the chair yourself. That's all you have to do.'

Larsen jumped up, gesticulating. 'For heaven's sake, Bayliss, are you crazy? Do you know what it's like to suddenly see yourself? All you want to do is run.'

'I realize that, but it's the worst thing you can do. Why whenever anyone grapples with a ghost does it always vanish instantly? Because forcibly occupying the same physical co-ordinates as the double jolts the psychic projector on to a single channel again. The two separate streams of retinal images coincide and fuse. You've got to try, Larsen. It may be quite an effort, but you'll cure yourself once and for all.'

Larsen shook his head stubbornly. 'The idea's insane.' To himself he added: I'd rather shoot the thing. Then he remembered the .38 in his suitcase, and the presence of the weapon gave him a stronger sense of security than all Bayliss's drugs and advice. The revolver was a simple symbol of aggression, and even if the phantom was only an intruder in his own mind, it gave that portion which still remained intact greater confidence, enough possibly to dissipate the double's power.

Eyes half closed with fatigue, he listened to Bayliss.

Half an hour later he went back to his chalet, found the revolver and hid it under a magazine in the letterbox outside the front door. It was too conspicuous to carry, and anyway might fire accidentally and injure him. Outside the front door it would be safely hidden and yet easily accessible, ready to mete out a little old-fashioned punishment to any double dealer trying to get into the game.

Two days later, with unexpected vengeance, the opportunity came.

Bayliss had driven into town to buy a new stylus for the stereogram, leaving Larsen to prepare lunch for them while he was away. Larsen pretended to resent the chore, but secretly he was glad of something to do. He was tired of hanging around the chalets while Bayliss watched him as if he were an experimental animal, eagerly waiting for the next crisis. With luck this might never come, if only to spite Bayliss, who had been having everything too much his own way.

After laying the table in Bayliss's kitchenette and getting plenty of ice ready for the martinis (alcohol was just the thing, Larsen readily decided, a wonderful C.N.S. depressant) he went back to his chalet and put on a clean shirt. On an impulse he decided to change his shoes and suit as well, and fished out the blue office serge and black oxfords he had worn on his way out to the desert. Not only were the associations of the cream suit and sports shoes unpleasant, but a complete change of costume might well forestall the double's reappearance, provide a fresh psychic image of himself powerful enough to suppress any wandering versions. Looking at himself in the mirror, he decided to carry the principle even farther. He switched on his shaver and cut away his moustache. Then he thinned out his hair and plastered it back smoothly across his scalp.

The transformation was effective. When Bayliss climbed out of his car and walked into the lounge he almost failed to recognize Larsen. He flinched back at the sight of the sleek-haired, dark-suited figure who stepped from behind the kitchen door.

'What the hell are you playing at?' he snapped at Larsen. 'This is no time for practical jokes.' He surveyed Larsen critically. 'You look like a cheap detective.'

Larsen guffawed. The incident put him in high spirits, and after several martinis he began to feel extremely buoyant. He talked away rapidly through the meal. Strangely, though, Bayliss seemed eager to get rid of him; he realized why shortly after he returned to his chalet. His pulse had quickened. He found himself prowling around nervously; his brain felt overactive and accelerated. The martinis had only been partly responsible for his elation. Now that they were wearing off he began to see the real agent—a stimulant Bayliss had given him in the hope of precipitating another crisis.

Larsen stood by the window, staring out angrily at Bayliss's chalet. The psychologist's utter lack of scruple outraged him. His fingers fretted nervously across the blind. Suddenly he felt like kicking the whole place down and speeding off. With its plywood-thin walls and match-box furniture the chalet was nothing more than a cardboard asylum. Everything that had happened there, the breakdowns and his nightmarish phantoms, had probably been schemed up by Bayliss deliberately.

Larsen noticed that the stimulant seemed to be extremely powerful. The take-off was sustained and unbroken. He tried hopelessly to relax, went into the bedroom and kicked his suitcase around, lit two cigarettes without realizing it.

Finally, unable to contain himself any longer, he slammed the front door back and stormed out across the apron, determined to have everything out with Bayliss and demand an immediate sedative.

Bayliss's lounge was empty. Larsen plunged through into the kitchen and bedroom, discovered to his annoyance that Bayliss was having a shower. He hung around in the lounge for a few moments, then decided to wait in his chalet.

Head down, he crossed the bright sunlight at a fast stride, and was only a few steps from the darkened doorway when he noticed that a man in a blue suit was standing there watching him.

Heart leaping, Larsen shrank back, recognizing the double even before he had completely accepted the change of costume, the smooth-shaven face with its altered planes. The man hovered indecisively, flexing his fingers, and appeared to be on the verge of stepping down into the sunlight.

Larsen was about ten feet from him, directly in line with Bayliss's door. He backed away, at the same time swinging to his left to the lee of the garage. There he stopped and pulled himself together. The double was still hesitating in the doorway, longer, he was sure, than he himself had done. Larsen looked at the face, repulsed, not so much by the absolute accuracy of the image, but by a strange, almost luminous pastiness that gave the double's features the waxy sheen of a corpse. It was this unpleasant gloss that held Larsen back—the double was an arm's length from the letterbox holding the ·38, and nothing could have induced Larsen to approach it.

He decided to enter the chalet and watch the double from behind. Rather than use the kitchen door, which gave access to the lounge on the double's immediate right, he turned to circle the garage and climb in through the bedroom window on the far side.

He was picking his way through a dump of old mortar and barbed wire behind the garage when he heard a voice call out:

'Larsen, you idiot, what do you think you're doing?'

It was Bayliss, leaning out of his bathroom window Larsen stumbled, found his balance and waved Bayliss back angrily. Bayliss merely shook his head and leaned farther out, drying his neck with a towel.

Larsen retraced his steps, signalling to Bayliss to keep quiet. He was crossing the space between the garage wall and the near corner of Bayliss's chalet when out of the side of his eye he noticed a dark-suited figure standing with its back to him a few yards from the garage door.

The double had moved! Larsen stopped, Bayliss forgotten, and watched the double warily. He was poised on the balls of his feet, as Larsen had been only a minute or so earlier, elbows up, hands waving defensively. His eyes were hidden, but he appeared to be looking at the front door of Larsen's chalet.

Automatically, Larsen's eyes also moved to the doorway.

The original blue-suited figure still stood there, staring out into the sunlight.

There was not one double now, but two.

For a moment Larsen stared helplessly at the two figures, standing on either side of the apron like half-animated dummies in a waxworks tableau.

The figure with its back to him swung on one heel and began to stalk rapidly towards him. He gazed sightlessly at Larsen, the sunlight exposing his face. With a jolt of horror Larsen recognized for the first time the perfect similarity of the double—the same plump cheeks, the same mole by the right nostril, the white upper lip with the same small razor cut where the moustache had been shaved away. Above all he recognized the man's state of shock, the nervous lips, the tension around the neck and facial muscles, the utter exhaustion just below the surface of the mask.

His voice strangled, Larsen turned and bolted.

He stopped running about two hundred yards out in the desert beyond the edge of the apron. Gasping for breath, he dropped to one knee behind a narrow sandstone outcropping and looked back at the chalets. The second double was making his way around the garage, climbing through the tangle of old wire. The other was crossing the space between the chalets. Oblivious of them both, Bayliss was struggling with the bathroom window, forcing it back so that he could see out into the desert.

Trying to steady himself, Larsen wiped his face on his jacket sleeve. So Bayliss had been right, although he had never anticipated that more than one image could be seen during any single attack. But in fact Larsen had spawned two in close succession, each at a critical phase during the last five minutes. Wondering whether to wait for the images to fade, Larsen remembered the revolver in the letterbox. However irrational, it seemed his only hope. With it he would be able to test the ultimate validity of the doubles.

The outcropping ran diagonally to the edge of the apron. Crouching forwards, he scurried along it, pausing at intervals to follow the scene. The two doubles were still holding their positions, though Bayliss had closed his window and disappeared.

Larsen reached the edge of the apron, which was built on a shallow table about a foot off the desert floor, and moved along its rim to where an old fifty-gallon drum gave him a vantage point. To reach the revolver he decided to go round the far side of Bayliss's chalet, where he would find his own doorway unguarded except for the double watching by the garage.

He was about to step forward when something made him look over his shoulder.

Running straight towards him along the outcropping, head down, hands almost touching the ground, was an enormous ratlike creature. Every ten or fifteen yards it paused for a moment, and looked out at the chalets, and Larsen caught a glimpse of its face, insane and terrified, another replica of his own.

'Larsen! Larsen!'

Bayliss stood by the chalet, waving out at the desert.

Larsen glanced back at the phantom hurtling towards him, now only thirty feet away, then jumped up and lurched helplessly across to Bayliss.

Bayliss caught him firmly with his hands. 'Larsen, what's the matter with you? Are you having an attack?'

Larsen gestured at the figures around him. 'Stop them, Bayliss, for God's sake,' he gasped. 'I can't get away from them.'

Bayliss shook him roughly. 'You can see *more* than one? Where are they? Show me.'

Larsen pointed at the two figures hovering luminously near the chalet, then waved limply in the direction of the desert. 'By the garage, and over there along the wall. There's another hiding along that ridge.'

Bayliss seized him by the arm. 'Come on, man, you've got to face up to them, it's no use running.' He tried to drag Larsen towards the garage, but Larsen slipped down on to the concrete.

'I can't, Bayliss, believe me. There's a gun in my letterbox. Get it for me. It's the only way.'

Bayliss hesitated, looking down at Larsen. 'All right. Try to hold on.'

Larsen pointed to the far corner of Bayliss's chalet. 'I'll wait over there for you.'

As Bayliss ran off he hobbled towards the corner. Halfway there he tripped across the remains of a ladder lying on the ground and twisted his right ankle between two of the rungs.

Clasping his foot, he sat down just as Bayliss appeared between the chalets, the revolver in his hand. He looked around for Larsen, who cleared his throat to call him.

Before he could open his mouth he saw the double who had followed him along the ridge leap up from behind the drum and stumble up to Bayliss across the concrete floor. He was dishevelled and exhausted, jacket almost off his shoulders, the tie knot under one ear. The image was still pursuing him, dogging his footsteps like an obsessed shadow.

Larsen tried to call to Bayliss again, but something he saw choked the voice in his throat.

Bayliss was looking at his double.

Larsen stood up, feeling a sudden premonition of terror. He tried to wave to Bayliss, but the latter was watching the double intently as it pointed to the figures near by, nodding to it in apparent agreement.

'Bayliss!'

The shot drowned his cry. Bayliss had fired somewhere between the garages, and the echo of the shot bounded among the chalets. The double was still beside him, pointing in all directions. Bayliss raised the revolver and fired again. The sound slammed across the concrete, making Larsen feel stunned and sick.

Now Bayliss too was seeing simultaneous images, not of himself but of Larsen, on whom his mind had been focusing for the past weeks. A repetition of Larsen stumbling over to him and pointing at the phantoms was being repeated in Bayliss's mind, at the exact moment when he had returned with the revolver and was searching for a target.

Larsen started to crawl away, trying to reach the corner. A third shot roared through the air, the flash reflected in the bathroom window.

He had almost reached the corner when he heard Bayliss shout. Leaning one hand against the wall, he looked back.

Mouth open, Bayliss was staring wildly at him, the

revolver clenched like a bomb in his hand. Beside him the blue-suited figure stood quietly, straightening its tie. At last Bayliss had realized he could see two images of Larsen, one beside him, the other twenty feet away against the chalet.

But how was he to know which was the real Larsen? Staring at Larsen, he seemed unable to decide.

Then the double by his shoulder raised one arm and pointed at Larsen, towards the corner wall to which he himself had pointed a minute earlier.

Larsen tried to shout, then hurled himself at the wall and pulled himself along it. Behind him Bayliss's feet came thudding across the concrete.

He heard only the first of the three shots.

For the first few days all went well.

'Keep away from windows and don't think about it,' Dr Neill told them. 'As far as you're concerned it was just another compulsion. At eleven thirty or twelve go down to the gym and throw a ball around, play some table-tennis. At two they're running a film for you in the Neurology theatre. Read the papers for a couple of hours, put on some records. I'll be down at six. By seven you'll be in a manic swing.'

'Any chance of a sudden blackout, Doctor?' Avery asked.

'Absolutely none,' Neill said. 'If you get tired, rest, of course. That's the one thing you'll probably have a little difficulty getting used to. Remember, you're still using only 3,500 calories, so your kinetic level—and you'll notice this most by day—will be about a third lower. You'll have to take things easier, make allowances. Most of these have been programmed in for you, but start learning to play chess, focus that inner eye.'

Gorrell leaned forward. 'Doctor,' he asked, 'if we want to, can we look out of the windows?'

Dr Neill smiled. 'Don't worry,' he said. 'The wires are cut. You couldn't go to sleep now if you tried.'

Neill waited until the three men had left the lecture room on their way back to the Recreation Wing and then stepped down from the dais and shut the door. He was a short, broad-shouldered man in his fifties, with a sharp, impatient mouth and small features. He swung a chair out of the front row and straddled it deftly.

'Well?' he asked.

Morley was sitting on one of the desks against the back wall, playing aimlessly with a pencil. At thirty he was the youngest member of the team working under

Neill at the Clinic, but for some reason Neill liked to talk to him.

He saw Neill was waiting for an answer and shrugged.

'Everything seems to be all right,' he said. 'Surgical convalescence is over. Cardiac rhythms and E.E.G. are normal. I saw the X-rays this morning and everything has sealed beautifully.'

Neill watched him quizzically. 'You don't sound as if you approve.'

Morley laughed and stood up. 'Of course I do.' He walked down the aisle between the desks, white coat unbuttoned, hands sunk deep in his pockets. 'No, so far you've vindicated yourself on every point. The party's only just beginning, but the guests are in damn good shape. No doubt about it. I thought three weeks was a little early to bring them out of hypnosis, but you'll probably be right there as well. Tonight is the first one they take on their own. Let's see how they are tomorrow morning.'

'What are you secretly expecting?' Neill asked wryly. 'Massive feed-back from the medulla?'

'No,' Morley said. 'There again the psychometric tests have shown absolutely nothing coming up at all. Not a single trauma.' He stared at the blackboard and then looked round at Neill. 'Yes, as a cautious estimate I'd say you've succeeded.'

Neill leaned forward on his elbows. He flexed his jaw muscles. 'I think I've more than succeeded. Blocking the medullary synapses has eliminated a lot of material I thought would still be there—the minor quirks and complexes, the petty aggressive phobias, the bad change in the psychic bank. Most of them have gone, or at least they don't show in the tests. However, they're the side targets, and thanks to you, John, and to everyone else in the team, we've hit a bull's eye on the main one.'

Morley murmured something, but Neill ran on in his

clipped voice. 'None of you realize it yet, but this is as big an advance as the step the first ichthyoid took out of the protozoic sea 300 million years ago. At last we've freed the mind, raised it out of that archaic sump called sleep, its nightly retreat into the medulla. With virtually one cut of the scalpel we've added twenty years to those men's lives.'

'I only hope they know what to do with them,' Morley commented.

'Come, John,' Neill snapped back. 'That's not an argument. What they do with the time is their responsibility anyway. They'll make the most of it, just as we've always made the most, eventually, of any opportunity given us. It's too early to think about it yet, but visualize the universal application of our technique. For the first time Man will be living a full twenty-four hour day, not spending a third of it as an invalid, snoring his way through an eight-hour peepshow of infantile erotica.'

Tired, Neill broke off and rubbed his eyes. 'What's worrying you?'

Morley made a small, helpless gesture with one hand. 'I'm not sure, it's just that I . . .' He played with the plastic brain mounted on a stand next to the blackboard. Reflected in one of the frontal whorls was a distorted image of Neill, with a twisted chinless face and vast domed cranium. Sitting alone among the desks in the empty lecture room he looked like an insane genius patiently waiting to take an examination no one could set him.

Morley turned the model with his finger, watched the image blur and dissolve. Whatever his doubts, Neill was probably the last person to understand them.

'I know all you've done is close off a few of the loops in the hypothalamus, and I realize the results are going to be spectacular. You'll probably precipitate the greatest social and economic revolution since the Fall.

But for some reason I can't get that story of Chekov's out of my mind—the one about the man who accepts a million-rouble bet that he can't shut himself up alone for ten years. He tries to, nothing goes wrong, but one minute before the time is up he deliberately steps out of his room. Of course, he's insane.'

'So?'

'I don't know. I've been thinking about it all week.'

Neill let out a light snort. 'I suppose you're trying to say that sleep is some sort of communal activity and that these three men are now isolated, exiled from the group unconscious, the dark oceanic dream. Is that it?'

'Maybe.'

'Nonsense, John. The further we hold back the unconscious the better. We're reclaiming some of the marshland. Physiologically sleep is nothing more than an inconvenient symptom of cerebral anoxaemia. It's not *that* you're afraid of missing, it's the dream. You want to hold on to your front-row seat at the peepshow.'

'No,' Morley said mildly. Sometimes Neill's aggressiveness surprised him; it was almost as if he regarded sleep itself as secretly discreditable, a concealed vice. 'What I really mean is that for better or worse Lang, Gorrell and Avery are now stuck with themselves. They're never going to be able to get away, not even for a couple of minutes, let alone eight hours. How much of yourself can you stand? Maybe you need eight hours off a day just to get over the shock of being yourself. Remember, you and I aren't always going to be around, feeding them with tests and films. What will happen if they get fed up with themselves?'

'They won't,' Neill said. He stood up, suddenly bored by Morley's questions. 'The total tempo of their lives will be lower than ours, these stresses and tensions won't begin to crystallize. We'll soon seem like a lot of manic-depressives to them, running round like dervishes half the day, then collapsing into a stupor the other half.'

He moved towards the door and reached out to the light switch. 'Well, I'll see you at six o'clock.'

They left the lecture room and started down the corridor together.

'What are you doing now?' Morley asked.

Neill laughed. 'What do you think?' he said. 'I'm going to get a good night's sleep.'

A little after midnight Avery and Gorrell were playing table-tennis in the floodlit gymnasium. They were competent players, and passed the ball backwards and forwards with a minimum of effort. Both felt strong and alert; Avery was sweating slightly, but this was due to the arc-lights blazing down from the roof—maintaining, for safety's sake, an illusion of continuous day—rather than to any excessive exertion of his own. The oldest of the three volunteers, a tall and somewhat detached figure, with a lean, closed face, he made no attempt to talk to Gorrell and concentrated on adjusting himself to the period ahead. He knew he would find no trace of fatigue, but as he played he carefully checked his respiratory rhythms and muscle tonus, and kept one eye on the clock.

Gorrell, a jaunty, self-composed man, was also subdued. Between strokes he glanced cautiously round the gymnasium, noting the hangar-like walls, the broad, polished floor, the shuttered skylights in the roof. Now and then, without realizing it, he fingered the circular trepan scar at the back of his head.

Out in the centre of the gymnasium a couple of armchairs and a sofa had been drawn up round a gramophone, and here Lang was playing chess with Morley, doing his section of night duty. Lang hunched forward over the chessboard. Wiry-haired and aggressive, with a sharp nose and mouth, he watched the pieces closely. He

had played regularly against Morley since he arrived at
the Clinic four months earlier, and the two were almost
equally matched, with perhaps a slight edge to Morley.
But tonight Lang had opened with a new attack and
after ten moves had completed his development and
begun to split Morley's defence. His mind felt clear and
precise, focused sharply on the game in front of him,
though only that morning had he finally left the cloudy
limbo of post-hypnosis through which he and the two
others had drifted for three weeks like lobotomized
phantoms.

Behind him, along one wall of the gymnasium, were
the offices housing the control unit. Over his shoulder he
saw a face peering at him through the circular observation window in one of the doors. Here, at constant alert,
a group of orderlies and interns sat around waiting by
their emergency trollies. (The end door, into a small
ward containing three cots, was kept carefully locked.)
After a few moments the face withdrew. Lang smiled at
the elaborate machinery watching over him. His transference on to Neill had been positive and he had absolute
faith in the success of the experiment. Neill had assured
him that, at worst, the sudden accumulation of meta-
bolites in his bloodstream might induce a mild torpor,
but his brain would be unimpaired.

'Nerve fibre, Robert,' Neill had told him time and
again, 'never fatigues. The brain cannot tire.'

While he waited for Morley to move he checked the
time from the clock mounted against the wall. Twelve
twenty. Morley yawned, his face drawn under the grey
skin. He looked tired and drab. He slumped down into
the armchair, face in one hand. Lang reflected how frail
and primitive those who slept would soon seem, their
minds sinking off each evening under the load of
accumulating toxins, the edge of their awareness worn
and frayed. Suddenly he realized that at that very mo-

ment Neill himself was asleep. A curiously disconcerting vision of Neill, huddled in a rumpled bed two floors above, his blood-sugar low, and his mind drifting, rose before him.

Lang laughed at his own conceit, and Morley retrieved the rook he had just moved.

'I must be going blind. What am I doing?'

'No,' Lang said. He started to laugh again. 'I've just discovered I'm awake.'

Morley smiled. 'We'll have to put that down as one of the sayings of the week.' He replaced the rook, sat up and looked across at the table-tennis pair. Gorrell had hit a fast backhand low over the net and Avery was running after the ball.

'They seem to be O.K. How about you?'

'Right on top of myself,' Lang said. His eyes flicked up and down the board and he moved before Morley caught his breath back.

Usually they went right through into the end-game, but tonight Morley had to concede on the twentieth move.

'Good,' he said encouragingly. 'You'll be able to take on Neill soon. Like another?'

'No. Actually the game bores me. I can see that's going to be a problem.'

'You'll face it. Give yourself time to find your legs.'

Lang pulled one of the Bach albums out of its rack in the record cabinet. He put a Brandenburg Concerto on the turntable and lowered the sapphire. As the rich, contrapuntal patterns chimed out he sat back, listening intently to the music.

Morley thought: Absurd. How fast can you run? Three weeks ago you were strictly a hep-cat.

The next few hours passed rapidly.

At one thirty they went up to the Surgery, where Morley and one of the interns gave them a quick physical, checking their renal clearances, heart rate and reflexes.

Dressed again, they went into the empty cafeteria for a snack and sat on the stools, arguing what to call this new fifth meal. Avery suggested 'Midfood', Morley 'Munch'.

At two they took their places in the Neurology theatre, and spent a couple of hours watching films of the hypno-drills of the past three weeks.

When the programme ended they started down for the gymnasium, the night almost over. They were still relaxed and cheerful; Gorrell led the way, playfully teasing Lang over some of the episodes in the films, mimicking his trance-like walk.

'Eyes shut, mouth open,' he demonstrated, swerving into Lang, who jumped nimbly out of his way. 'Look at you; you're doing it even now. Believe me, Lang, you're not awake, you're somnambulating.' He called back to Morley, 'Agreed, Doctor?'

Morley swallowed a yawn. 'Well, if he is, that makes two of us.' He followed them along the corridor, doing his best to stay awake, feeling as if he, and not the three men in front of him, had been without sleep for the last three weeks.

Though the Clinic was quiet, at Neill's orders all lights along the corridors and down the stairway had been left on. Ahead of them two orderlies checked that windows they passed were safely screened and doors were shut. Nowhere was there a single darkened alcove or shadow-trap.

Neill had insisted on this, reluctantly acknowledging a possible reflex association between darkness and sleep: 'Let's admit it. In all but a few organisms the association *is* strong enough to be a reflex. The higher mammals depend for their survival on a highly acute sensory apparatus, combined with a varying ability to store and classify information. Plunge them into darkness, cut off the flow of visual data to the cortex, and they're paralysed. Sleep is a defence reflex. It lowers the metabolic rate, conserves energy, increases the organism's survival-potential by merging it into it's habitat . . .'

On the landing halfway down the staircase was a wide, shuttered window that by day opened out on to the parkscape behind the Clinic. As he passed it Gorrell stopped. He went over, released the blind, then unlatched the shutter.

Still holding it closed, he turned to Morley, watching from the flight above.

'Taboo, Doctor?' he asked.

Morley looked at each of the three men in turn. Gorrell was calm and unperturbed, apparently satisfying nothing more sinister than an idle whim. Lang sat on the rail, watching curiously with an expression of clinical disinterest. Only Avery seemed slightly anxious, his thin face wan and pinched. Morley had an irrelevant thought : four a.m. shadow—they'll need to shave twice a day. Then : why isn't Neill here? He knew they'd make for a window as soon as they got the chance.

He noticed Lang giving him an amused smile and shrugged, trying to disguise his uneasiness.

'Go ahead, if you want to. As Neill said, the wires are cut.'

Gorrell threw back the shutter, and they clustered round the window and stared out into the night. Below, pewter-grey lawns stretched towards the pines and low hills in the distance. A couple of miles away on their left a neon sign winked and beckoned.

Neither Gorrell nor Lang noticed any reaction, and their interest began to flag within a few moments. Avery felt a sudden lift under the heart, then controlled himself. His eyes began to sift the darkness; the sky was clear and cloudless, and through the stars he picked out the narrow, milky traverse of the galactic rim. He watched it silently, letting the wind cool the sweat on his face and neck.

Morley stepped over to the window and leaned his elbows on the sill next to Avery. Out of the corner of his eye he carefully waited for any motor tremor—a fluttering eyelid, accelerated breathing—that would signal a reflex discharging. He remembered Neill's warning: 'In Man sleep is largely volitional, and the reflex is conditioned by habit. But just because we've cut out the hypothalamic loops regulating the flow of consciousness doesn't mean the reflex won't discharge down some other pathway. However, sooner or later we'll have to take the risk and give them a glimpse of the dark side of the sun.'

Morley was musing on this when something nudged his shoulder.

'Doctor,' he heard Lang say. 'Doctor Morley.'

He pulled himself together with a start. He was alone at the window. Gorrell and Avery were halfway down the next flight of stairs.

'What's up?' Morley asked quickly.

'Nothing,' Lang assured him. 'We're just going back to the gym.' He looked closely at Morley. 'Are you all right?'

Morley rubbed his face. 'God, I must have been asleep.' He glanced at his watch. Four twenty. They had been at the window for over fifteen minutes. All he could remember was leaning on the sill. 'And I was worried about *you*.'

Everybody was amused, Gorrell particularly. 'Doctor,' he drawled, 'if you're interested I can recommend you to a good narcotomist.'

After five o'clock they felt a gradual ebb of tonus from their arm and leg muscles. Renal clearances were falling and breakdown products were slowly clogging their tissues. Their palms felt damp and numb, the soles of their feet like pads of sponge rubber. The sensation was vaguely unsettling, allied to no feelings of mental fatigue.

The numbness spread. Avery noticed it stretching the skin over his cheekbones, pulling at his temples and giving him a slight frontal migraine. He doggedly turned the pages of a magazine, his hands like lumps of putty.

Then Neill came down, and they began to revive. Neill looked fresh and spruce, bouncing on the tips of his toes.

'How's the night shift going?' he asked briskly, walking round each one of them in turn, smiling as he sized them up. 'Feel all right?'

'Not too bad, Doctor,' Gorrell told him. 'A slight case of insomnia.'

Neill roared, slapped him on the shoulder and led the way up to the Surgery laboratory.

At nine, shaved and in fresh clothes, they assembled in the lecture room. They felt cool and alert again. The peripheral numbness and slight head torpor had gone as soon as the detoxication drips had been plugged in, and Neill told them that within a week their kidneys would have enlarged sufficiently to cope on their own.

All morning and most of the afternoon they worked on a series of I.Q., associative and performance tests. Neill kept them hard at it, steering swerving blips of light around a cathode screen, juggling with intricate numerical and geometric sequences, elaborating word-chains.

He seemed more than satisfied with the results.

'Shorter access times, deeper memory traces,' he pointed out to Morley when the three men had gone off at five for the rest period. 'Barrels of prime psychic marrow.' He gestured at the test cards spread out across the desk in his office. 'And you were worried about the Unconscious. Look at those Rorshachs of Lang's. Believe me, John, I'll soon have him reminiscing about his foetal experiences.'

Morley nodded, his first doubts fading.

Over the next two weeks either he or Neill was with the men continuously, sitting out under the floodlights in the centre of the gymnasium, assessing their assimilation of the eight extra hours, carefully watching for any symptoms of withdrawal. Neill carried everyone along, from one programme phase to the next, through the test periods, across the long hours of the interminable nights, his powerful ego injecting enthusiasm into every member of the unit.

Privately, Morley worried about the increasing emotional overlay apparent in the relationship between Neill and the three men. He was afraid they were becoming conditioned to identify Neill with the experiment. (Ring the meal bell and the subject salivates; but suddenly stop ringing the bell after a long period of conditioning and it temporarily loses the ability to feed itself. The hiatus barely harms a dog, but it might trigger disaster in an already oversensitized psyche.)

Neill was fully alert to this. At the end of the first two weeks, when he caught a bad head cold after sitting up all night and decided to spend the next day in bed, he called Morley into his office.

'The transference is getting much too positive. It needs to be eased off a little.'

'I agree,' Morley said. 'But how?'

'Tell them I'll be asleep for forty-eight hours,' Neill said. He picked up a stack of reports, plates and test cards and bundled them under one arm. 'I've deliberately overdosed myself with sedative to get some rest. I'm worn to a shadow, full fatigue syndrome, load-cells screaming. Lay it on.'

'Couldn't that be rather drastic?' Morley asked.

'They'll hate you for it.'

But Neill only smiled and went off to requisition an office near his bedroom.

That night Morley was on duty in the gymnasium from ten p.m. to six a.m. As usual he first checked that the orderlies were ready with their emergency trollies, read through the log left by the previous supervisor, one of the senior interns, and then went over to the circle of chairs. He sat back on the sofa next to Lang and leafed through a magazine, watching the three men carefully. In the glare of the arc-lights their lean faces had a sallow, cyanosed look. The senior intern had warned him that Avery and Gorrell might overtire themselves at table-tennis, but by eleven p.m. they stopped playing and settled down in the armchairs. They read desultorily and made two trips up to the cafeteria, escorted each time by one of the orderlies. Morley told them about Neill, but surprisingly none of them made any comment.

Midnight came slowly. Avery read, his long body hunched up in an armchair. Gorrell played chess against himself.

Morley dozed.

Lang felt restless. The gymnasium's silence and absence of movement oppressed him. He switched on the gramophone and played through a Brandenburg, analysing its theme-trains. Then he ran a word-association test on himself, turning the pages of a book and using the top right-hand corner words as the control list.

Morley leaned over. 'Anything come up?' he asked.

'A few interesting responses.' Lang found a note-pad and jotted something down. 'I'll show them to Neill in the morning—or whenever he wakes up.' He gazed up pensively at the arc-lights. 'I was just speculating. What do you think the next step forward will be?'

'Forward where?' Morley asked.

Lang gestured expansively. 'I mean up the evolutionary slope. Three hundred million years ago we became air-breathers and left the seas behind. Now we've taken the next logical step forward and eliminated sleep. What's next?'

Morley shook his head. 'The two steps aren't analogous. Anyway, in point of fact you haven't left the primeval sea behind. You're still carrying a private replica of it around as your bloodstream. All you did was encapsulate a necessary piece of the physical environment in order to escape it.'

Lang nodded. 'I was thinking of something else. Tell me, has it ever occurred to you how completely death-orientated the psyche is?'

Morley smiled. 'Now and then,' he said, wondering where this led.

'It's curious,' Lang went on reflectively. 'The pleasure-pain principle, the whole survival-compulsion apparatus of sex, the Super-Ego's obsession with tomorrow—most of the time the psyche can't see farther than its own tombstone. Now why has it got this strange fixation? For one very obvious reason.' He tapped the air with his forefinger. 'Because every night it's given a pretty convincing reminder of the fate in store for it.'

'You mean the black hole,' Morley, suggested wryly. 'Sleep?'

'Exactly. It's simply a psuedo-death. Of course, you're not aware of it, but it must be terrifying.' He frowned. 'I don't think even Neill realizes that, far from being restful, sleep is a genuinely traumatic experience.'

So that's it, Morley thought. The great father analyst has been caught napping on his own couch. He tried to decide which were worse—patients who knew a lot of psychiatry, or those who only knew a little.

'Eliminate sleep,' Lang was saying, 'and you also eliminate all the fear and defence mechanisms erected

round it. Then, at last, the psyche has a chance to orien-
tate towards something more valid.'

'Such as . . .?' Morley asked.

'I don't know. Perhaps . . . Self?'

'Interesting,' Morley commented. It was three ten a.m.
He decided to spend the next hour going through Lang's
latest test cards.

He waited a discretionary five minutes, then stood up
and walked over to the surgery office.

Lang hooked an arm across the back of the sofa and
watched the orderly room door.

'What's Morley playing at?' he asked. 'Have either of
you seen him anywhere?'

Avery lowered his magazine. 'Didn't he go off into the
orderly room?'

'Ten minutes ago,' Lang said. 'He hasn't looked in
since. There's supposed to be someone on duty with us
continuously. Where is he?'

Gorrell, playing solitaire chess, looked up from his
board. 'Perhaps these late nights are getting him down.
You'd better wake him before Neill finds out. He's probably fallen asleep over a batch of your test cards.'

Lang laughed and settled down on the sofa. Gorrell
reached out to the gramophone, took a record out of the
rack and slid it on to the turntable.

As the gramophone began to hum Lang noticed how
silent and deserted the gymnasium seemed. The Clinic
was always quiet, but even at night a residual ebb and
flow of sound—a chair dragging in the orderly room, a
generator charging under one of the theatres—eddied
through and kept it alive.

Now the air was flat and motionless. Lang listened
carefully. The whole place had the dead, echoless feel of
an abandoned building.

He stood up and strolled over to the orderly room. He

knew Neill discouraged casual conversation with the control crew, but Morley's absence puzzled him.

He reached the door and peered through the window to see if Morley was inside.

The room was empty.

The light was on. Two emergency trollies stood in their usual place against the wall near the door, a third was in the middle of the floor, a pack of playing cards strewn across its deck, but the group of three or four interns had gone.

Lang hesitated, reached down to open the door, and found it had been locked.

He tried the handle again, then called out over his shoulder :

'Avery. There's nobody in here.'

'Try next door. They're probably being briefed for tomorrow.'

Lang stepped over to the surgery office. The light was off but he could see the white enamelled desk and the big programme charts round the wall. There was no one inside.

Avery and Gorrell were watching him.

'Are they in there?' Avery asked.

'No,' Lang turned the handle. 'The door's locked.'

Gorrell switched off the gramophone and he and Avery came over. They tried the two doors again.

'They're here somewhere,' Avery said. 'There must be at least one person on duty.' He pointed to the end door. 'What about that one?'

'Locked,' Lang said. '69 always has been. I think it leads down to the basement.'

'Let's try Neill's office,' Gorrell suggested. 'If they aren't in there we'll stroll through to Reception and try to leave. This must be some trick of Neill's.'

There was no window in the door to Neill's office. Gorrell knocked, waited, knocked again more loudly.

Lang tried the handle, then knelt down. 'The light's off,' he reported.

Avery turned and looked round at the two remaining doors out of the gymnasium, both in the far wall, one leading up to the cafeteria and the Neurology wing, the other into the car park at the rear of the Clinic.

'Didn't Neill hint that he might try something like this on us?' he asked. 'To see whether we can go through a night on our own.'

'But Neill's asleep,' Lang objected. 'He'll be in bed for a couple of days. Unless . . .'

Gorrell jerked his head in the direction of the chairs. 'Come on. He and Morley are probably watching us now.'

They went back to their seats.

Gorrell dragged the chess stool over to the sofa and set up the pieces. Avery and Lang stretched out in armchairs and opened magazines, turning the pages deliberately. Above them the banks of arc-lights threw their wide cones of light down into the silence.

The only noise was the slow left-right, left-right motion of the clock.

Three fifteen a.m.

The shift was imperceptible. At first a slight change of perspective, a fading and regrouping of outlines. Somewhere a focus slipped, a shadow swung slowly across a wall, its angles breaking and lengthening. The motion was fluid, a procession of infinitesimals, but gradually its total direction emerged.

The gymnasium was shrinking. Inch by inch, the walls were moving inwards, encroaching across the periphery of the floor. As they shrank towards each other their features altered: the rows of skylights below the ceiling blurred and faded, the power cable running along the base of the wall merged into the skirting board, the

*square baffles of the air vents vanished into the grey
distemper.*

*Above, like the undersurface of an enormous lift, the
ceiling sank towards the floor . . .*

Gorrell leaned his elbows on the chessboard, face sunk in
his hands. He had locked himself in a perpetual check,
but he continued to shuttle the pieces in and out of one
of the corner squares, now and then gazing into the air
for inspiration, while his eyes roved up and down the
walls around him.

Somewhere, he knew, Neill was watching him.

He moved, looked up and followed the wall opposite
him down to the far corner, alert for the telltale signs of
a retractable panel. For some while he had been trying to
discover Neill's spy-hole, but without any success. The
walls were blank and featureless; he had twice covered
every square foot of the two facing him, and apart from
the three doors there appeared to be no fault or aperture
of even the most minute size anywhere on their surface.

After a while his left eye began to throb painfully, and
he pushed away the chessboard and lay back. Above him
a line of fluorescent tubes hung down from the ceiling,
mounted in checkered plastic brackets that diffused the
light. He was about to comment on his search for the
spy-hole to Avery and Lang when he realized that any
one of them could conceal a microphone.

He decided to stretch his legs, stood up and sauntered
off across the floor. After sitting over the chessboard for
half an hour he felt cramped and restless, and would
have enjoyed tossing a ball up and down, or flexing his
muscles on a rowing machine. But annoyingly no re-
creational facilities, apart from the three armchairs and
the gramophone, had been provided.

He reached the end wall and wandered round, listening for any sound from the adjacent rooms. He was

beginning to resent Neill spying on him and the entire keyhole conspiracy, and he noted with relief that it was a quarter past three : in under three hours it would all be over.

The gymnasium closed in. Now less than half its original size, its walls bare and windowless, it was a vast, shrinking box. The sides slid into each other, merging along an abstract hairline, like planes severing in a multi-dimensional flux. Only the clock and a single door remained ...

Lang had discovered where the microphone was hidden.

He sat forward in his chair, cracking his knuckles until Gorrell returned, then rose and offered him his seat. Avery was in the other armchair, feet up on the gramophone.

'Sit down for a bit,' Lang said. 'I feel like a stroll.'

Gorrell lowered himself into the chair. 'I'll ask Neill if we can have a ping-pong table in here. It should help pass the time and give us some exercise.'

'A good idea,' Lang agreed. 'If we can get the table through the door. I doubt if there's enough room in here, even if we moved the chairs right up against the wall.'

He walked off across the floor, surreptitiously peering through the orderly room window. The light was on, but there was still no one inside.

He ambled over to the gramophone and paced up and down near it for a few moments. Suddenly he swung round and caught his foot under the flex leading to the wall socket.

The plug fell out on to the floor. Lang left it where it lay, went over and sat down on the arm of Gorrell's chair.

'I've just disconnected the microphone,' he confided.

Gorrell looked round carefully. 'Where was it?'

Lang pointed. 'Inside the gramophone.' He laughed

softly. 'I thought I'd pull Neill's leg. He'll be wild when he realizes he can't hear us.'

'Why do you think it was in the gramophone?' Gorrell asked.

'What better place? Besides, it couldn't be anywhere else. Apart from in there.' He gestured at the light bowl suspended from the centre of the ceiling. 'It's empty except for the two bulbs. The gramophone is the obvious place. I had a feeling it was there, but I wasn't sure until I noticed we had a gramophone, but no records.'

Gorrell nodded sagely.

Lang moved away, chuckling to himself.

Above the door of Room 69 the clock ticked on at three fifteen.

The motion was accelerating. What had once been the gymnasium was now a small room, seven feet wide, a tight, almost perfect cube. The walls plunged inwards, along colliding diagonals, only a few feet from their final focus...

Avery noticed Gorrell and Lang pacing around his chair. 'Either of you want to sit down yet?' he asked.

They shook their heads. Avery rested for a few minutes and then climbed out of the chair and stretched himself.

'Quarter past three,' he remarked, pressing his hands against the ceiling. 'This is getting to be a long night.'

He leaned back to let Gorrell pass him, and then started to follow the others round the narrow space between the armchair and the walls.

'I don't know how Neill expects us to stay awake in this hole for twenty-four hours a day,' he went on. 'Why haven't we got a television set in here? Even a radio would be something.'

They sidled round the chair together, Gorrell, followed

by Avery, with Lang completing the circle, their shoulders beginning to hunch, their heads down as they watched the floor, their feet falling into the slow, leaden rhythm of the clock.

This, then, was the manhole: a narrow, vertical cubicle, a few feet wide, six deep. Above, a solitary, dusty bulb gleamed down from a steel grille. As if crumbling under the impetus of their own momentum, the surface of the walls had coarsened, the texture was that of stone, streaked and pitted ...

Gorrell bent down to loosen one of his shoelaces and Avery bumped into him sharply, knocking his shoulder against the wall.

'All right?' he asked, taking Gorrell's arm. 'This place is a little overcrowded. I can't understand why Neill ever put us in here.'

He leaned against the wall, head bowed to prevent it from touching the ceiling, and gazed about thoughtfully.

Lang stood squeezed into the corner next to him, shifting his weight from one foot to the other.

Gorrell squatted down on his heels below them.

'What's the time?' he asked.

'I'd say about three fifteen,' Lang offered. 'More or less.'

'Lang,' Avery asked, 'where's the ventilator here?'

Lang peered up and down the walls and across the small square of ceiling. 'There must be one somewhere.' Gorrell stood up and they shuffled about, examining the floor between their feet.

'There may be a vent in the light grille,' Gorrell suggested. He reached up and slipped his fingers through the cage, running them behind the bulb.

'Nothing there. Odd. I should have thought we'd use the air in here within half an hour.'

'Easily,' Avery said. 'You know, there's something——'

Just then Lang broke in. He gripped Avery's elbow.

'Avery,' he asked. 'Tell me. How did we get here?'

'What do you mean, get here? We're on Neill's team.'

Lang cut him off. 'I know that.' He pointed at the floor. 'I mean, in here.'

Gorrell shook his head. 'Lang, relax. How do you think? Through the door.'

Lang looked squarely at Gorrell, then at Avery.

'What door?' he asked calmly.

Gorrell and Avery hesitated, then swung round to look at each wall in turn, scanning it from floor to ceiling. Avery ran his hands over the heavy masonry, then knelt down and felt the floor, digging his fingers at the rough stone slabs. Gorrell crouched beside him, scrabbling at the thin seams of dirt.

Lang backed out of their way into a corner, and watched them impassively. His face was calm and motionless, but in his left temple a single vein fluttered insanely.

When they finally stood up, staring at each other unsteadily, he flung himself between them at the opposite wall.

'Neill! Neill!' he shouted. He pounded angrily on the wall with his fists. 'Neill! Neill!'

Above him the light began to fade.

Morley closed the door of the surgery office behind him and went over to the desk. Though it was three fifteen a.m., Neill was probably awake, working on the latest material in the office next to his bedroom. Fortunately that afternoon's test cards, freshly marked by one of the interns, had only just reached his in-tray.

Morley picked out Lang's folder and started to sort through the cards. He suspected that Lang's responses to some of the key words and suggestion triggers lying disguised in the question forms might throw illuminating sidelights on to the real motives behind his equation of sleep and death.

The communicating door to the orderly room opened and an intern looked in.

'Do you want me to take over in the gym, Doctor?'

Morley waved him away. 'Don't bother. I'm going back in a moment.'

He selected the cards he wanted and began to initial his withdrawals. Glad to get away from the glare of the arclights, he delayed his return as long as he could, and it was three twenty-five a.m. when he finally left the office and stepped back into the gymnasium.

The men were sitting where he had left them. Lang watched him approach, head propped comfortably on a cushion. Avery was slouched down in his armchair, nose in a magazine, while Gorrell hunched over the chess-board, hidden behind the sofa.

'Anybody feel like coffee?' Morley called out, deciding they needed some exercise.

None of them looked up or answered. Morley felt a flicker of annoyance, particularly at Lang, who was staring past him at the clock.

Then he saw something that made him stop.

Lying on the polished floor ten feet from the sofa was a chess piece. He went over and picked it up. The piece was the black king. He wondered how Gorrell could be playing chess with one of the two essential pieces of the game missing when he noticed three more pieces lying on the floor near by.

His eyes moved to where Gorrell was sitting.

Scattered over the floor below the chair and sofa was the rest of the set. Gorrell was slumped over the stool. One of his elbows had slipped and the arm dangled between his knees, knuckles resting on the floor. The other hand supported his face. Dead eyes peered down at his feet.

Morley ran over to him, shouting: 'Lang! Avery! Get the orderlies!'

He reached Gorrell and pulled him back off the stool. 'Lang!' he called again.

Lang was still staring at the clock, his body in the stiff, unreal posture of a waxworks dummy.

Morley let Gorrell loll back on to the sofa, leaned over and glanced at Lang's face.

He crossed to Avery, stretched out behind the magazine, and jerked his shoulder. Avery's head bobbed stiffly. The magazine slipped and fell from his hands, leaving his fingers curled in front of his face.

Morley stepped over Avery's legs to the gramophone. He switched it on, gripped the volume control and swung it round to full amplitude.

Above the orderly room door an alarm bell shrilled out through the silence.

'Weren't you with them?' Neill asked sharply.

'No,' Morley admitted. They were standing by the door of the emergency ward. Two orderlies had just dismantled the electro-therapy unit and were wheeling the console away on a trolley. Outside in the gymnasium a quiet, urgent traffic of nurses and interns moved past. All but a single bank of arc-lights had been switched off, and the gymnasium seemed like a deserted stage at the end of a performance.

'I slipped into the office to pick up a few test cards,' he explained. 'I wasn't gone more than ten minutes.'

'You were supposed to watch them continuously,' Neill snapped. 'Not wander off by yourself whenever you felt like it. What do you think we had the gym and this entire circus set up for?'

It was a little after five thirty a.m. After working hopelessly on the three men for a couple of hours, he was close to exhaustion. He looked down at them, lying inertly in their cots, canvas sheets buckled up to their chins. They had barely changed, but their eyes were open and unblinking, and their faces had the empty, reflexless look of psychic zero.

An intern bent over Lang, thumbing a hypodermic. Morley stared at the floor. 'I think they would have gone anyway.'

'How can you say that?' Neill clamped his lips together. He felt frustrated and impotent. He knew Morley was probably right—the three men were in terminal withdrawal, unresponsive to either insulin or electrotherapy, and a vice-tight catatonic seizure didn't close in out of nowhere—but as always refused to admit anything without absolute proof.

He led the way into his office and shut the door.

'Sit down.' He pulled a chair out for Morley and prowled off round the room, slamming a fist into his palm.

'All right, John. What is it?'

Morley picked up one of the test cards lying on the desk, balanced it on a corner and spun it between his fingers. Phrases swam through his mind, tentative and uncertain, like blind fish.

'What do you want me to say?' he asked. 'Reactivation of the infantile imago? A regression into the great, slumbering womb? Or to put it more simply still—just a fit of pique?'

'Go on.'

Morley shrugged. 'Continual consciousness is more than the brain can stand. Any signal repeated often enough eventually loses its meaning. Try saying the word "sleep" fifty times. After a point the brain's self-awareness dulls. It's no longer able to grasp who or why it is, and it rides adrift.'

'What do we do then?'

'Nothing. Short of re-scoring all the way down to

Lumbar 1. The central nervous system can't stand narcotomy.'

Neill shook his head. 'You're lost,' he said curtly. 'Juggling with generalities isn't going to bring those men back. First, we've got to find out what happened to them, what they actually felt and saw.'

Morley frowned dubiously. 'That jungle is marked "private". Even if you do, is a psychotic's withdrawal drama going to make any sense?'

'Of course it will. However insane it seems to us, it was real enough to them. If we know the ceiling fell in or the whole gym filled with ice-cream or turned into a maze, we've got something to work on.' He sat down on the desk. 'Do you remember that story of Chekov's you told me about?'

' "The Bet"? Yes.'

'I read it last night. Curious. It's a lot nearer what you're really trying to say than you know.' He gazed round the office. 'This room in which the man is penned for ten years symbolizes the mind driven to the furthest limits of self-awareness ... Something very similar happened to Avery, Gorrell and Lang. They must have reached a stage beyond which they could no longer contain the idea of their own identity. But far from being unable to grasp the idea, I'd say that they were conscious of nothing else. Like the man in the spherical mirror, who can only see a single gigantic eye staring back at him.'

'So you think their withdrawal is a straightforward escape from the eye, the overwhelming ego?'

'Not escape,' Neill corrected. 'The psychotic never escapes from anything. He's much more sensible. He merely readjusts reality to suit himself. Quite a trick to learn, too. The room in Chekov's story gives me an idea as to how they might have re-adjusted. Their particular equivalent of this room was the gym. I'm beginning to realize it was a mistake to put them in there—all those lights blazing down, the huge floor, high walls. They merely exaggerate the sensation of overload. In fact the gym might easily have become an external projection of their own egos.'

Neill drummed his fingers on the desk. 'My guess is that at this moment they're either striding around in there the size of hundred-foot giants, or else they've cut it down to their own dimensions. More probably that They've just pulled the gym in on themselves.'

Morley grinned bleakly. 'So all we've got to do now is pump them full of honey and apomorphine and coax them out. Suppose they refuse?'

'They won't,' Neill said. 'You'll see.'

There was a rap on the door. An intern stuck his head through.

'Lang's coming out of it, Doctor. He's calling for you.'

Neill bounded out.

Morley followed him into the ward.

Lang was lying in his cot, body motionless under the canvas sheet. His lips were parted slightly. No sound came from them but Morley, bending over next to Neill, could see his hyoid bone vibrating in spasms.

'He's very faint,' the intern warned.

Neill pulled up a chair and sat down next to the cot. He made a visible effort of concentration, flexing his shoulders. He bent his head close to Lang's and listened.

Five minutes later it came through again.

Lang's lips quivered. His body arched under the sheet, straining at the buckles, and then subsided.

'Neill ... Neill,' he whispered. The sounds, thin and strangled, seemed to be coming from the bottom of a well. 'Neill ... Neill ... Neill ...'

Neill stroked his forehead with a small, neat hand.

'Yes, Bobby,' he said gently. His voice was feather-soft, caressing. 'I'm here, Bobby. You can come out now.'

At low tide, their eggs buried at last in the broken sand below the dunes, the turtles began their return journey to the sea. To Conrad Foster, watching beside his uncle from the balustrade along the beach road, there seemed little more than fifty yards to the safety of the slack water. The turtles laboured on, their dark humps hidden among the orange crates and the drifts of kelp washed up from the sea. Conrad pointed to the flock of gulls resting on the submerged sandbank in the mouth of the estuary. The birds had been staring out to sea, as if uninterested in the deserted shoreline where the old man and the boy waited by the rail, but at this small movement of Conrad's a dozen white heads turned together.

'They've seen them . . .' Conrad let his arm fall to the rail. 'Uncle Theodore, do you think——?'

His uncle gestured with the stick at a car moving along the road a quarter of a mile away. 'It could have been the car.' He took his pipe from his mouth as a cry came from the sandbank. The first flight of gulls rose into the air and began to turn like a scythe towards the shore. 'Here they come.'

The turtles had emerged from the shelter of the debris by the tideline. They advanced across the sheet of damp sand that sloped down to the sea, the screams of the gulls tearing at the air over their heads.

Involuntarily Conrad moved away towards the row of chalets and the deserted tea garden on the outskirts of the town. His uncle held his arm. The turtles were being picked from the shallow water and dropped on the sand, then dismembered by a dozen beaks.

Within barely a minute of their arrival the birds began to rise from the beach. Conrad and his uncle had not been the only spectators of the gulls' brief feast. A small party of some dozen men stepped down from their vantage point among the dunes and moved along the sand, driving the last of the birds away from the turtles. The men were all elderly, well into their sixties and seventies, and wore singlets and cotton trousers rolled to their knees. Each carried a canvas bag and a wooden gaff tipped by a steel blade. As they picked up the shells they cleaned them with swift, practised movements and dropped them into their bags. The wet sand was streaked with blood, and soon the old men's bare feet and arms were covered with the bright stains.

'I dare say you're ready to move.' Uncle Theodore looked up at the sky, following the gulls back to the estuary. 'Your aunt will have something waiting for us.'

Conrad was watching the old men. As they passed, one of them raised his ruby-tipped gaff in greeting. 'Who are they?' he asked as his uncle acknowledged the salute.

'Shell collectors—they come here in the season. These shells fetch a good price.'

They set off towards the town, Uncle Theodore moving at a slow pace with his stick. As he waited Conrad glanced back along the beach. For some reason the sight of the old men streaked with the blood of the slaughtered turtles was more disturbing than the viciousness of the seagulls. Then he remembered that he himself had probably set off the birds.

The sounds of a truck overlaid the fading cries of the gulls as they settled themselves on the sandbank. The old men had gone, and the incoming tide was beginning to wash the stained sand. They reached the crossing by the first of the chalets. Conrad steered his uncle to the traffic island in the centre of the road. As they waited for the truck to pass he said, 'Uncle, did you notice the birds never touched the sand?'

The truck roared past them, its high pantechnicon blocking off the sky. Conrad took his uncle's arm and moved forward. The old man plodded on, rooting his stick in the sandy tarmac. Then he flinched back, the pipe falling from his mouth as he shouted at the sports car swerving towards them out of the dust behind the truck. Conrad caught a glimpse of the driver's white knuckles on the rim of the steering wheel, a frozen face behind the windshield as the car, running down its own brakes, began to slide sideways across the road. Conrad started to push the old man back but the car was on them, bursting across the traffic island in a roar of dust.

The hospital was almost empty. During the first days Conrad was glad to lie motionlessly in the deserted ward, watching the patterns of light reflected on to the ceiling from the flowers on the window-sill, listening to the few sounds from the orderly room beyond the swing doors. At intervals the nurse would come and look at him. Once, when she bent down to straighten the cradle over his legs, he noticed that she was not a young woman but even older than his aunt, despite her slim figure and the purple rinse in her hair. In fact, all the nurses and orderlies who tended him in the empty ward were elderly, and obviously regarded Conrad more as a child than a youth of seventeen, treating him to a mindless and amiable banter as they moved about the ward.

Later, when the pain from his amputated leg roused him from this placid second sleep, Nurse Sadie at last began to look at his face. She told him that his aunt had come to visit him each day after the accident, and that she would return the following afternoon.

'. . . Theodore—Uncle Theodore . . .?' Conrad tried to sit up but an invisible leg, as dead and heavy as a mastodon's, anchored him to the bed. 'Mr Foster . . . my uncle. Did the car . . .?'

'Missed him by yards, dear. Or let's say inches.' Nurse Sadie touched his forehead with a hand like a cool bird. 'Only a scratch on his wrist where the windshield cut it.

My, the glass we took out of you, though, you looked as if you'd jumped through a greenhouse!'

Conrad moved his head away from her fingers. He searched the rows of empty beds in the ward. 'Where is he? Here . . .?'

'At home. Your aunt's looking after him, he'll be right as rain.'

Conrad lay back, waiting for Nurse Sadie to go away so that he could be alone with the pain in his vanished leg. Above him the surgical cradle loomed like a white mountain. Strangely, the news that Uncle Theodore had escaped almost unscathed from the accident left Conrad without any sense of relief. Since the age of five, when the deaths of his parents in an air disaster had left him an orphan, his relationship with his aunt and uncle had been, if anything, even closer than that he would have had with his mother and father, their affection and loyalties more conscious and constant. Yet he found himself thinking not of his uncle, nor of himself, but of the approaching car. With its sharp fins and trim it had swerved towards them like the gulls swooping on the turtles, moving with the same rush of violence. Lying in the bed with the cradle over him Conrad remembered the turtles labouring across the wet sand under their heavy carapaces, and the old men waiting for them among the dunes.

Outside, the fountains played among the gardens of the empty hospital, and the elderly nurses walked in pairs to and fro along the shaded pathways.

The next day, before his aunt's visit, two doctors came to see Conrad. The older of the two, Dr Nathan, was a slim grey-haired man with hands as gentle as Nurse Sadie's. Conrad had seen him before, and remembered him from the first confused hours of his admission to the hospital. A faint half-smile always hung about Dr

Nathan's mouth, like the ghost of some forgotten pleasantry.

The other physician, Dr Knight, was considerably younger, and by comparison seemed almost the same age as Conrad. His strong, square-jawed face looked down at Conrad with a kind of jocular hostility. He reached for Conrad's wrist as if about to jerk the youth from his bed on to the floor.

'So this is young Foster?' He peered into Conrad's eyes. 'Well, Conrad, I won't ask how you're feeling.'

'No . . .' Conrad nodded uncertainly.

'No, what?' Dr Knight smiled at Nathan, who was hovering at the foot of the bed like an aged flamingo in a dried-up pool. 'I thought Dr Nathan was looking after you very well.' When Conrad murmured something, shy of inviting another retort, Dr Knight sped on : 'Isn't he? Still, I'm more interested in your future, Conrad. This is where I take over from Dr Nathan, so from now on you can blame me for everything that goes wrong.'

He pulled up a metal chair and straddled it, flicking out the tails of his white coat with a flourish. 'Not that anything will. Well?'

Conrad listened to Dr Nathan's feet tapping the polished floor. He cleared his throat. 'Where is everyone else?'

'You've noticed?' Dr Knight glanced across at his colleague. 'Still, you could hardly fail to.' He stared through the window at the empty grounds of the hospital. 'It's true, there is hardly anyone here.'

'A compliment to us, Conrad, don't you think?' Dr Nathan approached the bed again. The smile that hovered around his lips seemed to belong to another face.

'Yeesss . . .' Dr Knight drawled. 'Of course, no one will have explained to you, Conrad, but this isn't a hospital in quite the usual sense.'

'What——?' Conrad began to sit up, dragging at the cradle over his leg. 'What do you mean?'

Dr Knight raised his hands. 'Don't misinterpret me, Conrad. Of course this is a hospital, an advanced surgical unit, in fact, but it's also something more than a hospital, as I intend to explain.'

Conrad watched Dr Nathan. The older physician was gazing out of the window, apparently at the fountains, but for once his face was blank, the smile absent.

'In what way?' Conrad asked guardedly. 'Is it something to do with me?'

Dr Knight spread his hands in an ambiguous gesture. 'In a sense, yes. But we'll talk about this tomorrow. We've taxed you enough for the present.'

He stood up, his eyes still examining Conrad, and placed his hands on the cradle. 'We've a lot of work to do on this leg, Conrad. In the end, when we've finished, you'll be pleasantly surprised at what we can achieve here. In return, perhaps you can help us—we hope so, don't we, Dr Nathan?'

Dr Nathan's smile, like a returning wraith, hovered once again about his thin lips. 'I'm sure Conrad will be only too keen.'

As they reached the door Conrad called them back.

'What is it, Conrad?' Dr Knight waited by the next bed.

'The driver—the man in the car. What happened to him? Is he here?'

'As a matter of fact he is, but . . .' Dr Knight hesitated, then seemed to change course. 'To be honest, Conrad, you won't be able to see him. I know the accident was almost certainly his fault——'

'No!' Conrad shook his head. 'I don't want to blame him . . . we stepped out behind the truck. Is he here?'

'The car hit the steel pylon on the traffic island, then went on through the sea wall. The driver was killed on the beach. He wasn't much older than you, Conrad, in a way he may have been trying to save you and your uncle.'

Conrad nodded, remembering the white face like a scream behind the windshield.

Dr Knight turned towards the door. Almost *sotto voce* he added : 'And you'll see, Conrad, he can still help you.'

At three o'clock that afternoon Conrad's uncle appeared. Seated in a wheelchair, and pushed by his wife and Nurse Sadie, he waved cheerily to Conrad with his free hand as he entered the ward. For once, however, the sight of Uncle Theodore failed to raise Conrad's spirits. He had been looking forward to the visit, but his uncle had aged ten years since the accident and the sight of these three elderly people, one of them partially crippled, coming towards him with their smiling faces only reminded him of his isolation in the hospital.

As he listened to his uncle, Conrad realized that this isolation was merely a more extreme version of his own position, and that of all young people, outside the walls of the hospital. As a child Conrad had known few friends of his own age, for the single reason that children were almost as rare as centenarians had been a hundred years earlier. He had been born into a middle-aged world, one moreover where middle age itself was for ever moving, like the horizons of a receding universe, farther and farther from its original starting point. His aunt and uncle, both of them nearly sixty, represented the median line. Beyond them was the immense super-annuated army of the elderly, filling the shops and streets of the seaside town, their slow rhythms and hesitant walk overlaying everything like a grey veil.

By contrast, Dr Knight's self-confidence and casual air, however brusque and aggressive, quickened Conrad's pulse.

Towards the end of the visit, when his aunt had strolled to the end of the ward with Nurse Sadie to view the fountains, Conrad said to his uncle, 'Dr Knight told me he could do something for my leg.'

'I'm sure he can, Conrad.' Uncle Theodore smiled encouragingly, but his eyes watched Conrad without moving. 'These surgeons are clever men; it's amazing what they can do.'

'And your hand, Uncle?' Conrad pointed to the dressing that covered his uncle's left forearm. The hint of irony in his uncle's voice reminded him of Dr Knight's studied ambiguities. Already he sensed that people were taking sides around him.

'This hand?' His uncle shrugged. 'It's done me for nearly sixty years, a missing finger won't stop me filling my pipe.' Before Conrad could speak he went on: 'But that leg of yours is a different matter, you'll have to decide for yourself what to have done with it.'

Just before he left he whispered to Conrad, 'Rest yourself well, lad. You may have to run before you can walk.'

Two days later, promptly at nine o'clock, Dr Knight came to see Conrad. Brisk as ever, he came to the point immediately.

'Now, Conrad,' he began, replacing the cradle after his inspection. 'it's a month since your last stroll by the beach, time to get you out of here and back on your own feet again. What do you say?'

'*Feet?*' Conrad repeated. He managed a slight laugh. 'Do you mean that as a figure of speech?'

'No, I mean it literally.' Dr Knight drew up a chair. 'Tell me, Conrad, have you ever heard of restorative surgery? It may have been mentioned at school.'

'In biology—transplanting kidneys and that sort of thing. Older people have it done. Is that what you're going to do to my leg?'

'Whoa! Hold your horses. Let's get a few things straight first. As you say, restorative surgery goes back about fifty years, when the first kidney grafts were made, though for years before that corneal grafting was commonplace. If you accept that blood is a tissue the principle is even older—you had a massive blood transfusion after the accident, and later when Dr Nathan amputated the crushed knee and shinbone. Nothing surprising about that, is there?'

Conrad waited before answering. For once Dr Knight's tone had become defensive, as if he were already, by some sort of extrapolation, asking the questions to which he feared Conrad might subsequently object.

'No,' Conrad replied. 'Nothing at all.'

'Obviously, why should there be? Though it's worth bearing in mind that many people have refused to accept blood transfusions, even though it meant certain death. Apart from their religious objections, many of them felt that the foreign blood polluted their own bodies.' Dr Knight leaned back, scowling to himself. 'One can see their point of view, but remember that our bodies are almost completely composed of alien materials. We don't stop eating, do we, just to preserve our own absolute identity?' Dr Knight laughed here. 'That would be egotism run riot. Don't you agree?'

When Dr Knight glanced at him, as if waiting for an answer, Conrad said, 'More or less.'

'Good. And, of course, in the past most people have taken your point of view. The substitution of a healthy kidney for a diseased one doesn't in any way diminish your own integrity, particularly if your life is saved. What counts is your own continuing identity. By their very structure the individual parts of the body serve a larger physiological whole, and the human consciousness is great enough to provide any sense of unity.

'Now, no one ever seriously disputed this, and fifty years ago a number of brave men and women, many of them physicians, voluntarily gave their healthy organs to others who needed them. Sadly, all these efforts failed after a few weeks as a result of the so-called immunity reaction. The host body, even though it was dying, still fought against the graft as it would against any alien organism.'

Conrad shook his head. 'I thought they'd solved this immunity problem.'

'In time, yes—it was a question of biochemistry rather than any fault in the surgical techniques used. Eventually the way became clear, and every year tens of thousands of lives were saved—people with degenerative diseases of the liver, kidneys, alimentary tract, even portions of the heart and nervous system, were given transplated organs. The main problem was where to obtain them—you may be willing to donate a kidney, but you can't give away your liver or the mitral valve in your heart. Luckily a great number of people willed their organs posthumously—in fact, it's now a condition of admission to a public hospital that in the event of death any parts of one's body may be used in restorative surgery. Originally the only organs that were banked were those of the thorax and abdomen, but today we have reserves of literally every tissue in the human body, so that whatever the surgeon requires is available, whether it's a complete lung or a few square centimetres of some specialized epithelium.'

As Dr Knight sat back Conrad pointed at the ward around him. 'This hospital . . . this is where it happens?'

'Exactly, Conrad. This is one of the hundreds of institutes we have today devoted to restorative surgery. As you'll understand, only a small percentage of the patients who come here are cases such as yours. The greatest application of restorative surgery has been for geriatric purposes, that is, for prolonging life in the aged.'

Dr Knight nodded deliberately as Conrad sat up. 'Now you'll understand, Conrad, why there have always been so many elderly people in the world around you. The reason is simple—by means of restorative surgery we've been able to give people who would normally die in their sixties and seventies a second span of life. The average life span has risen from sixty-five half a century ago to something close to ninety-five.'

'Doctor ... the driver of the car. I don't know his name. You said he could still help me.'

'I meant what I said, Conrad. One of the problems of restorative surgery is that of supply. In the case of the elderly it's straightforward, if anything there's an excess of replacement materials over the demand. Apart from a few generalized degenerative conditions, most elderly people are faced with the failure of perhaps no more than one organ, and every fatality provides a reserve of tissues that will keep twenty others alive for as many years. However, in the case of the young, particularly in your age group, the demand exceeds supply a hundred-fold. Tell me, Conrad, quite apart from the driver of the car, how do you feel in principle about undergoing restorative surgery?'

Conrad looked down at the bedclothes. Despite the cradle, the asymmetry of his limbs was too obvious to miss. 'It's hard to say. I suppose I ...'

'The choice is yours, Conrad. Either you wear a pros-thetic limb—a metal support that will give you endless discomfort for the rest of your life, and prevent you from running and swimming, from all the normal move-ments of a young man—or else you have a leg of flesh and blood and bone.'

Conrad hesitated. Everything Dr Knight had said tallied with all he had heard over the years about re-storative surgery—the subject was not taboo, but seldom discussed, particularly in the presence of children. Yet he was sure that this elaborate résumé was the prologue to some far more difficult decision he would have to take. 'When do you do this—tomorrow?'

'Good God, no!' Dr Knight laughed involuntarily, then let his voice roll on, dispelling the tension between them. 'Not for about two months, it's a tremendously complex piece of work. We've got to identify and tag all the nerve endings and tendons, then prepare an elaborate bone graft. For at least a month you'll be wearing an artificial limb—believe me, by the end you'll be looking forward to getting back on a real leg. Now, Conrad, can I assume that in general you're quite willing? We need both your permission and your uncle's.'

'I think so. I'd like to talk to Uncle Theodore. Still, I know I haven't really got any choice.'

'Sensible man.' Dr Knight held out his hand. As Conrad reached to take it he realized that Dr Knight was deliberately showing him a faint hairline scar that ran around the base of his thumb and then disappeared inside the palm. The thumb seemed wholly part of the hand, and yet detached from it.

'That's right,' Dr Knight told him. 'A small example of restorative surgery. Done while I was a student. I lost the top joint after infecting it in the dissecting room. The entire thumb was replaced. It's served me well; I couldn't really have taken up surgery without it.' Dr Knight traced the faint scar across his palm for Conrad. 'There are slight differences of course, the articulation for one thing—this one is a little more dexterous than my own used to be, and the nail is a different shape, but otherwise it feels like me. There's also a certain altruistic pleasure that one is keeping alive part of another human being.'

'Dr Knight—the driver of the car. You want to give me his leg?'

'That's true, Conrad. I should have to tell you, anyway, the patient must agree to the donor—people are naturally hesitant about being grafted to part of a criminal or psychopath. As I explained, for someone of your age it's not easy to find the appropriate donor . . .'

'But, Doctor——' For once Dr Knight's reasoning bewildered Conrad. 'There must be someone else. It's not that I feel any grudge against him, but . . . There's some other reason, isn't there?'

Dr Knight nodded after a pause. He walked away from the bed, and for a moment Conrad wondered if he was about to abandon the entire case. Then he turned on his heel and pointed through the window.

'Conrad, while you've been here has it occurred to you to wonder why this hospital is empty?'

Conrad gestured at the distant walls. 'Perhaps it's too large. How many patients can it take?'

'Over two thousand. It *is* large, but fifteen years ago, before I came here, it was barely big enough to deal with the influx of patients. Most of them were geriatric cases —men and women in their seventies and eighties who were having one or more vital organs replaced. There were immense waiting lists, many of the patients were trying to pay hugely inflated fees—bribes, if you like— to get in.'

'Where have they all gone?'

'An interesting question—the answer in part explains why you're here, Conrad, and why we're taking a special interest in your case. You see, Conrad, about ten or twelve years ago hospital boards all over the country noticed that admission rates were starting to fall off. To begin with they were relieved, but the decline has gone on each year, until now the rate of admission is down to about one per cent of the previous intake. And most of these patients are surgeons and physicians, or members of the nursing staff.'

'But, Doctor—if they're not coming here . . .' Conrad

found himself thinking of his aunt and uncle. 'If they won't come here that means they're choosing to . . .'

Dr Knight nodded. 'Exactly, Conrad. They're choosing to die.'

A week later, when his uncle came to see him again, Conrad explained to him Dr Knight's proposition. They sat together on the terrace outside the ward, looking out over the fountains at the deserted hospital. His uncle still wore a surgical mitten over his hand, but otherwise had recovered from the accident. He listened silently to Conrad.

'None of the old people are coming any more, they're lying at home when they fall ill and . . . waiting for the end. Dr Knight says there's no reason why in many cases restorative surgery shouldn't prolong life more or less indefinitely.'

'A sort of life. How does he think you can help them, Conrad?'

'Well, he believes that they need an example to follow, a symbol if you like. Someone like myself who's been badly hurt in an accident right at the start of his life might make them accept the real benefits of restorative surgery.'

'The two cases are hardly similar,' his uncle mused. 'However . . . How do you feel about it?'

'Dr Knight's been completely frank. He's told me about those early cases where people who'd had new organs and limbs literally fell apart when the seams failed. I suppose he's right. Life should be preserved—you'd help a dying man if you found him on the pavement, why not in some other case? Because cancer or bronchitis are less dramatic——'

'I understand, Conrad.' His uncle raised a hand. 'But why does he think older people are refusing surgery?'

'He admits he doesn't know. He feels that as the

average age of the population rises there's a tendency for the old people to dominate society and set its mood. Instead of having a majority of younger people around them they see only the aged like themselves. The one way of escape is death.'

'It's a theory. One thing—he wants to give you the leg of the driver who hit us. That seems a strange touch. A little ghoulish.'

'No, it's the whole point—he's trying to say that once the leg is grafted it becomes part of *me*.' Conrad pointed to his uncle's mitten. 'Uncle Theodore, that hand. You lost two of the fingers. Dr Knight told me. Are you going to have them restored?'

His uncle laughed. 'Are you trying to make me your first convert, Conrad?'

Two months later Conrad re-entered the hospital to undergo the restorative surgery for which he had been waiting during his convalescence. On the previous day he accompanied his uncle on a short visit to friends who lived in the retirement hostels to the north-west of the town. These pleasant single-storey buildings in the chalet style, built by the municipal authority and let out to their occupants at a low rent, constituted a considerable fraction of the town's area. In the three weeks he had been ambulant Conrad seemed to have visited every one. The artificial limb with which he had been fitted was far from comfortable, but at Dr Knight's request his uncle had taken Conrad to all the acquaintances he knew.

Although the purpose of these visits was to identify Conrad to as many of the elderly residents as possible before he returned to the hospital—the main effort at conversion would come later, when the new limb was in place—Conrad had already begun to doubt whether Dr Knight's plan would succeed. Far from arousing any hostility, Conrad's presence elicited nothing but sympathy and goodwill from the aged occupants of the residential hostels and bungalows. Wherever he went the old people would come down to their gates and talk to him, wishing him well with his operation. At times, as he acknowledged the smiles and greetings of the grey-haired men and women watching on all sides from their balconies and gardens, it seemed to Conrad that he was the only young person in the entire town.

'Uncle, how do you explain the paradox?' he asked as they limped along together on their rounds, Conrad supporting his weight on two stout walking sticks. 'They want me to have a new leg but they won't go to the hospital themselves.'

'But you're young, Conrad, a mere child to them. You're having returned to you something that is your right: the ability to walk and run and dance. Your life isn't being prolonged beyond its natural span.'

'Natural span?' Conrad repeated the phrase wearily. He rubbed the harness of his leg beneath his trousers. 'In some parts of the world the natural life span is still little more than forty. Isn't it relative?'

'Not entirely, Conrad. Not beyond a certain point.' Although he had faithfully guided Conrad about the town, his uncle seemed reluctant to pursue the argument.

They reached the entrance to one of the residential estates. One of the town's many undertakers had opened a new office, and in the shadows behind the leaded windows Conrad could see a prayer-book on a mahogany stand and discreet photographs of hearses and mausoleums. However veiled, the proximity of the office to the retirement homes disturbed Conrad as much as if a line of freshly primed coffins had been laid out along the pavement ready for inspection.

His uncle merely shrugged when Conrad mentioned this. 'The old take a realistic view of things, Conrad.

They don't fear or sentimentalize death in quite the way the younger people do. In fact, they have a very lively interest in the matter.'

As they stopped outside one of the chalets he took Conrad's arm. 'A word of warning here, Conrad. I don't want to shock you, but you're about to meet a man who intends to put his opposition to Dr Knight into practice. Perhaps he'll tell you more in a few minutes than I or Dr Knight could in ten years. His name is Matthews, by the way, Dr James Matthews.'

'Doctor?' Conrad repeated. 'Do you mean a doctor of medicine?'

'Exactly. One of the few. Still, let's wait until you meet him.'

They approached the chalet, a modest two-roomed dwelling with a small untended garden dominated by a tall cypress. The door opened as soon as they touched the bell. An elderly nun in the uniform of a nursing order let them in with a brief greeting. A second nun, her sleeves rolled, crossed the passage to the kitchen with a porcelain pail. Despite their efforts, there was an unpleasant smell in the house which the lavish use of disinfectant failed to conceal.

'Mr Foster, would you mind waiting a few minutes. Good morning, Conrad.'

They waited in the dingy sitting-room. Conrad studied the framed photographs over the rolltop desk. One was of a birdlike, grey-haired woman, whom he took to be the deceased Mrs Matthews. The other was an old matriculation portrait of a group of students.

Eventually they were shown into the small rear bedroom. The second of the two nuns had covered the equipment on the bedside table with a sheet. She straightened the coverlet on the bed and then went out into the hall.

Resting on his sticks, Conrad stood behind his uncle as

the latter peered down at tne occupant of the bed. The acid odour was more pungent and seemed to emanate directly from the bed. When his uncle beckoned him forward, Conrad at first failed to find the shrunken face of the man in the bed. The grey cheeks and hair had already merged into the unstarched sheets covered by the shadows from the curtained windows.

'James, this is Elizabeth's boy, Conrad.' His uncle pulled up a wooden chair. He motioned to Conrad to sit down. 'Dr Matthews, Conrad.'

Conrad murmured something, aware of the blue eyes that had turned to look at him. What surprised him most about the dying occupant of the bed was his comparative youth. Although in his middle sixties, Dr Matthews was twenty years younger than the majority of the tanants in the estate.

'He's grown into quite a lad, don't you think, James?' Uncle Theodore remarked.

Dr Matthews nodded, as if only half interested in their visit. His eyes were on the dark cypress in the garden. 'He has,' he said at last.

Conrad waited uncomfortably. The walk had tired him, and his thigh seemed raw again. He wondered if they would be able to call for a taxi from the house.

Dr Matthews turned his head. He seemed to be able to look at Conrad and his uncle with a blue eye on each of them. 'Who have you got for the boy?' he asked in a sharper voice. 'Nathan is still there, I believe . . .'

'One of the younger men, James. You probably won't know him, but he's a good fellow. Knight.'

'Knight?' The name was repeated with only a faint hint of comment. 'And when does the boy go in?'

'Tomorrow. Don't you, Conrad?'

Conrad was about to speak when he noticed that a faint simpering was coming from the man in the bed. Suddenly exhausted by this bizarre scene, and under the impression that the dying physician's macabre humour was directed at himself, Conrad rose in his chair, rattling his sticks together. 'Uncle, could I wait outside . . .?'

'My boy——' Dr Matthews had freed his right hand from the bed. 'I was laughing at your uncle, not at you. He always had a great sense of humour. Or none at all. Which is it, Theo?'

'I see nothing funny, James. Are you saying I shouldn't have brought him here?'

Dr Matthews lay back. 'Not at all—I was there at his beginning, let him be here for my end . . .' He looked at Conrad again. 'I wish you the best, Conrad. No doubt you wonder why I don't accompany you to the hospital.'

'Well, I . . .' Conrad began, but his uncle held his shoulder.

'James, it's time for us to be leaving. I think we can take the matter as understood.'

'Obviously we can't.' Dr Matthews raised a hand again, frowning at the slight noise. 'I'll only be a moment, Theo, but if I don't tell him no one will, certainly not Dr Knight. Now, Conrad, you're seventeen?'

When Conrad nodded Dr Matthews went on : 'At that age, if I remember, life seems to stretch on for ever. One is probably living as close to eternity as is possible. As you get older, though, you find more and more that everything worthwhile has finite bounds, by and large those of time—from ordinary things to the most important ones, your marriage, children and so on, even life itself. The hard lines drawn around things give them their identity. Nothing is brighter than the diamond.'

'James, you've had enough——'

'Quiet, Theo.' Dr Matthews raised his head, almost managing to sit up. 'Perhaps, Conrad, you would explain to Dr Knight that it is just because we value our lives so much that we refuse to diminish them. There are a thousand hard lines drawn between you and me, Conrad, differences of age, character and experience, differences of *time*. You have to earn these distinctions for yourself. You can't borrow them from anyone else, least of all from the dead.'

Conrad looked round as the door opened. The older of the nuns stood in the hall outside. She nodded to his uncle. Conrad settled his limb for the journey home, waiting for Uncle Theodore to make his goodbyes to Dr Matthews. As the nun stepped towards the bed he saw on the train of her starched gown a streak of blood.

Outside they plodded together past the undertakers, Conrad heaving himself along on his sticks. As the old people in the gardens waved to them Uncle Theodore said, 'I'm sorry he seemed to laugh at you, Conrad. It wasn't meant.'

'Was he there when I was born?'

'He attended your mother. I thought it only right that you should see him before he died. Why he thought it so funny I can't understand.'

Almost six months later to the day, Conrad Foster walked down towards the beach road and the sea. In the sunlight he could see the high dunes above the beach, and beyond them the gulls sitting out on the submerged sandbank in the mouth of the estuary. The traffic along the beach road was busier than he remembered from his previous visit, and the sand picked up by the wheels of the speeding cars and trucks drifted in clouds across the fields.

Conrad moved at a good pace along the road, testing his new leg to the full. During the past four months the bonds had consolidated themselves with the minimum of pain, and the leg was, if anything, stronger and more resilient than his own had ever been. At times, when he walked along without thinking, it seemed to stride ahead with a will of its own.

Yet despite its good service, and the fulfilment of all that Dr Knight had promised him for it, Conrad had failed to accept the leg. The thin hairline of the surgical scar that circled his thigh above the knee was a frontier that separated the two more absolutely than any physical barrier. As Dr Matthews had stated, its presence seemed to diminish him, in some way subtracting rather than adding to his own sense of identity. This feeling had grown with each week and month as the leg itself recovered its strength. At night they would lie together like silent partners in an uneasy marriage.

In the first month after his recovery Conrad had agreed to help Dr Knight and the hospital authorities in the second stage of their campaign to persuade the elderly to undergo restorative surgery rather than throw away their lives, but after Dr Matthew's death Conrad decided to take no further part in the scheme. Unlike Dr Knight, he realized that there was no real means of persuasion, and that only those on their deathbeds, such as Dr Matthews, were prepared to argue the matter at all. The others simply smiled and waved from their quiet gardens.

In addition, Conrad knew that his own growing uncertainty over the new limb would soon be obvious to their sharp eyes. A large scar now disfigured the skin above the shin-bone, and the reasons were plain. Injuring it while using his uncle's lawnmower, he had deliberately let the wound fester, as if this act of self-mutilation might symbolize the amputation of the limb. However, it seemed only to thrive on this blood letting.

A hundred yards away was the junction with the beach road, the fine sand lifting off the surface in the light breeze. A quarter of a mile away a line of vehicles approached at speed, the drivers of the cars at the rear trying to overtake two heavy trucks. Far away, in the estuary, there was a faint cry from the sea. Although tired, Conrad found himself breaking into a run. Somewhere a familiar conjunction of events was guiding him back towards the place of his accident.

As he reached the corner the first of the trucks was drawing close to him, the driver flashing his headlamps as Conrad hovered on the curb, eager to get back to the pedestrian island with its freshly painted pylon.

Above the noise he saw the gulls rising into the air above the beach, and heard their harsh cries as the white sword drew itself across the sky. As it swept down over the beach the old men with their metal-tipped gaffs were moving from the road to their hiding-place among the dunes.

The truck thudded past him, the grey dust stinging his face as the slipstream whipped across it. A heavy saloon car rolled by, overtaking the truck and the other cars pressing behind it. The gulls began to dive and scream across the beach, and Conrad darted through the dust into the centre of the road and ran forward into the cars as they swerved towards him.